THE TEXAS TATTLER

All The News You Need To Know...And More!

We all know the story of Alex Montoya. The poor boy who pulled himself up by his bootstraps to become an ultrasuccessful businessman. Now, money practically falls from his fingertips. But does everyone also remember why he left Maverick County in the first place? Rumor had it that he'd been fooling around with the Huntingtons' beloved daughter. A no-no if we ever heard one.

Could it be any coincidence, then, that since Alex's return, he has one Rebecca Huntington working for him? Well, we use the term "working" quite loosely. Surely this rich man's daughter isn't actually cleaning Montoya's house? Unless it's just a matter of changing the sheets...

Any chance that the millionaire from the wrong side of the tracks and the privileged princess fallen on hard times have a future? We can't wait to find out.

Dear Reader,

I have always loved writing about family, just as I love being part of so many different types of families. There's the one I was born into, with two sisters, a brother and my parents. There's the one I created with my husband and our son (as well as an assortment of family pets whom we treat as family!). There's the one I created with my closest friends, soul sisters who are different in wonderful ways but who are, at heart, one with me. And then there's the wonderful family you form with your fellow writers…in this case my new family at Silhouette Books.

As a serious hermit, those myriad relationships have always been very important to me. And yet, sometimes they're in conflict. Wants and needs of one family will, on occasion, conflict with the wants and needs of another.

I think that's what appealed to me about writing *Lone Star Seduction*. Not only are there sisterly bonds of deep and abiding friendship, there are families in conflict, just as we experience in real life. Picking a path through those landmines of emotion and need is a process that never grows old for me. And finding a way to resolve the conflicts inherent in familial relationships never ceases to fascinate.

If family is a particular love of yours, welcome to the final book in the TEXAS CATTLEMAN'S CLUB, the conclusion to a series of books that, at its core, is all about friends and family in conflict…and struggling to find that happily-ever-after resolution. They're stories that take these special people from mere friendship to the everlasting bond of a true family.

Enjoy!

Day Leclaire

DAY LECLAIRE

LONE STAR SEDUCTION

Silhouette®

Desire

Published by Silhouette Books
America's Publisher of Contemporary Romance

Special thanks and acknowledgment to Day Leclaire
for her contribution to the Texas Cattleman's Club:
Maverick County Millionaires miniseries.

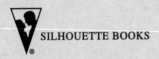

SILHOUETTE BOOKS

ISBN-13: 978-0-373-76983-4

Recycling programs
for this product may
not exist in your area.

LONE STAR SEDUCTION

Copyright © 2009 by Harlequin Books S.A.

Visit Silhouette Books at www.eHarlequin.com

Printed in U.S.A.

Books by Day Leclaire

Silhouette Desire

DAY LECLAIRE

USA TODAY bestselling author Day Leclaire is described by Harlequin as "one of our most popular writers ever!" Day's tremendous worldwide popularity has made her a member of Harlequin's "Five Star Club," with sales of well over five million books. She is a three-time winner of both a Colorado Award of Excellence and a Golden Quill Award. She's won *RT Book Reviews* Career Achievement and Love and Laughter Awards, a Holt Medallion and a Booksellers Best Award. She has also received an impressive ten nominations for the prestigious Romance Writers of America RITA® Award. Day's romances touch the heart and make you care about her characters as much as she does. In Day's own words, "I adore writing romances, and can't think of a better way to spend each day." For more information, visit Day on her Web site, www.dayleclaire.com.

To my new family at Silhouette Desire, and
all the wonderful authors who contributed to the
TEXAS CATTLEMAN'S CLUB series. Many thanks.

Texas Cattleman's Club:
Maverick County Millionaires

One

It was inevitable.

Rebecca Huntington knew it was only a matter of time before her path and Alejandro Montoya's collided. In this case, literally. Stepping from the brilliant Texas sunlight into the elegant interior of the Texas Cattleman's Club, she walked straight into his arms.

He caught her. Of course, he caught her. He had the reflexes of a cat, no doubt thanks to his years on the soccer field. For one brief, insane second her body gave, imprinting itself against his like a bittersweet memory. How many years had it been since they'd made love as though there were no yesterday, no tomorrow, only this moment of endless joy? She'd thought she'd found the love of a lifetime. Instead, he'd taken her innocence and ended their relationship with breathtaking cruelty, something it had taken her years to get over. And here she was, back in his arms, shades of that long-ago love affair haunting her still.

"Excuse me." His voice caressed her, the passage of years having deepened the slight Latino intonation, making it even more delicious than when they'd dated. "If you'll let go of me, I can leave."

Part of her wanted to cringe and pull away. But she refused to allow him the satisfaction of seeing how much he could still affect her. She released her grip on him—why in the world were her hands grasping his crisp, white shirt?—and held her ground.

The sunlight streaming in through the open doorway hit him square in the face, leaving hers in shadow. She could only be grateful for that fact when she saw the expression in his rich brown eyes—one of acute dislike, bordering on loathing. She didn't understand it, had never understood how their affair could have gone so hideously wrong. Nor could she understand why every part of her responded to him as though they were still one.

He towered over her five-foot-six frame by a full eight inches, though she managed to gain a small advantage with three-inch heels. High, sweeping cheekbones emphasized his deep-set eyes and framed a straight nose and full, sensuous mouth. She'd lost herself in that mouth, one skilled in the art of giving a woman pleasure beyond description.

She didn't dare let him know how deeply he'd affected her. Somehow, someway, he'd use the information. And it wouldn't be to her advantage. "If you'll step back, I'll be on my way," she said.

He held his position for an extra second. And then she saw it. A blistering hint of those communal memories drifted into his expression, a fading echo of the passion they'd once shared. Like an ember hidden deep within a banked fire, her touch uncovered the white-hot blaze of his passion. Alex felt something for her. Still. Some small trace of the hunger and desire they'd once shared lived within him. And then it was gone, the sweetness fading beneath the acrid burn of bitter discord. But it was too late. She knew. He'd managed to bury his reaction with impressive speed, but she hadn't mistaken it. The flame had been there.

Just as a matching flame burned within her.

As though aware of how much he'd given away, he stepped backward and gestured her in with a gracious nod. Both he and his sister, Alicia, had impeccable manners. Their mother, Carmen, who had also been the Huntington's one-time housekeeper, had insisted on it. Forcing herself to move, Rebecca swept past without giving him another look. Recovering her equilibrium was an entirely different matter. She could feel his gaze like a fine-tuned laser frying a hole between her shoulder blades as she continued on her way.

She made a beeline for the Texas Cattleman's Club Café, relieved to see that her luncheon date and best friend, Kate Thornton—now Brody—hadn't yet arrived. It gave Rebecca a moment to sit and pull herself together. The waiter, Richie, who often served her and who had memorized the preferences of all the regulars, brought over unsweetened iced tea and a dish of lemon.

He greeted her with a broad smile. "Lots of action today," he said in an undertone.

She grasped the topic like a lifeline—anything that would help erase Alex Montoya from her mind…and heart. "Interesting," she said, taking a long, refreshing sip of tea. "What sort of action?"

"Some sort of meeting among our newer mavericks. Maybe they're planning a coup to replace the old guard," he joked. He looked up in time to catch a reprimanding glance from the hostess and segued smoothly back into the role of waiter. "I assume someone's joining you?"

"Kate Brody."

"Ah, yes. Unsweetened tea during the summer, boiling-hot coffee during the winter. I think her husband is one of those participating in the meeting."

Rebecca shook her head with a grin, her tension easing. "How do you know so much about what's going on, Richie?"

He leaned in, keeping his voice low. "Pays to know, Ms. Huntington. Better tips. And sometimes I pick up suggestions on how to get ahead in life, like from Mr. Montoya." Richie's eyes shone with hero worship. "He's always helping out the staff."

She stiffened. "I…I didn't realize."

And she hadn't. Granted, she'd been out of the loop while living in Houston and learning how to run a retail business. But where had she been the past year since she moved back to Somerset? Working her fingers to the bone getting her lingerie shop, Sweet Nothings, established and in the black. And during her few precious hours off, she got together with her friends. If she were honest, she'd admit that she'd been careful not to listen to gossip about one of the TCC's newest members, especially since the other recent members—like the Brody brothers, Darius Franklin and Justin Dupree—were at odds with Alex. But maybe it was time to pay closer attention. Especially now that Justin was poised to become Alex's brother-in-law.

Kate appeared in the doorway of the café just then, scanning the tables for Rebecca. Tall and lanky, she was beautifully turned out in one of the chic pantsuits the two of them had selected on their Houston shopping spree. In one short day, her best friend had gone from country-bland to Southern sophisticate and Rebecca couldn't be more delighted, especially since it had led to Kate's then employer—now husband—tripping right over his tongue and into her bed.

Spotting Rebecca, Kate broke into a broad smile and worked her way around the blue-and-yellow floral-chintz tables. "So, what's got you all worked up?" she asked as they exchanged hugs.

Was it that obvious? Not good. Rebecca took a stab at innocent denial. "I have no idea what you're talking about. I'm fine."

Kate waved that aside with a sweep of her hand. "That won't wash with me, and you know it. Something's wrong and—" She broke off, her gaze arrowing across the room. "Okay, that explains it. I wondered when you two would finally bump into each other, and today must have been the day."

Rebecca didn't need to look to know precisely who Kate was talking about. Alex had returned to the club with a file in hand. He must have been on his way to his car to retrieve it when they'd run into each other. She could feel his presence like a low-level buzz of electricity. "Would it surprise you to hear that it didn't go well?"

"No," she retorted crisply. "The man is incredibly difficult. If Lance had his way, Montoya never would have been invited to join the club."

"Money talks."

Kate smiled thinly. "Well, he has plenty of that, doesn't he? Amazing, considering he used to be the groundskeeper here. I just hope the rumors aren't true."

Rebecca eyed her friend in concern. "What rumors?"

Kate hesitated. "You must know he has ties to El Gato."

"Paulo Rodriguez, sure. They're childhood friends." Understanding dawned and she inhaled sharply. "People think Alex made his money from drug trafficking?" She dismissed the suggestion out of hand. "No way. Not a chance. Not Alex."

"Not trafficking," Kate replied. "Shall we say…investing in some of El Gato's activities."

Rebecca shook her head, adamant. "Sorry, I don't

believe it. I can say a lot about Alex—plenty of it bad—but not that. Never that."

Richie arrived just then with Kate's coffee. Apparently, the crisp November weather had been the deciding factor on the choice of beverage. Based on Kate's appreciative grin, he'd chosen right. "You ladies ready to order? Our special today is the mahi-mahi with our homemade zesty dill pesto. It's really good."

"I'm sold," Kate announced.

"Make that two," Rebecca agreed.

"Coming right up." Richie jotted down a quick note and then gave a soft whistle. "Now there's a sight I never thought I'd live to see. Alex Montoya and Lance Brody shaking hands. Even weirder, the earth hasn't stopped spinning."

Startled, Rebecca glanced over her shoulder and saw that Alex had been joined by Kate's husband, Lance, his brother Mitch, and fellow frat brother, Kevin Novak. The three men were indeed shaking hands, though she could see the coolness and tension in their body language. As she watched, Justin Dupree and Darius Franklin joined the group, bringing all six of the newest, hottest TCC members together.

Rebecca couldn't contain her curiosity. "Okay, what's all that about?"

Kate frowned. Checking to confirm that Richie had moved out of earshot, she explained, "Some hush-hush meeting about the recent arson fires. Lance is there because the first fire was at Brody Oil and Gas. Since the other was at El Diablo, Alex needed to be present for the meeting, as well."

Rebecca stiffened. Of course, she'd heard about the fires. She wasn't that far out of the loop. And she knew that arson had been suspected. "It's been confirmed? They're certain both fires were arson?"

"That's my understanding. Why?"

Rebecca shot her friend an apologetic look, knowing how rough recent events had been on Kate's husband and his family. "Dad insists the fires were accidental, particularly the Montoya blaze."

"No offense, Becca, but how would your father know?" Kate asked. "Unless he's in on the investigation—and last I heard he didn't work for Darius's security firm—he wouldn't have anything to base his opinion on, other than secondhand information or gossip."

"Fair enough," Rebecca conceded, taking a cooling sip of her iced tea.

"Plus, they think they have a suspect."

Startled, she returned her glass to the table. "Who?"

Kate grimaced. "I was afraid you were going to ask me that. Lance told me the name." Her brow wrinkled as she struggled to remember. "Cantry?"

Rebecca froze. "Could it have been Gentry?"

Kate shrugged. "That's possible. Why?" She leaned forward and asked urgently, "Do you know this man, Becca?"

"I don't know anyone named Cantry," she temporized.

"But you do know a Gentry." It wasn't a question.

Rebecca nodded. "My father hired a new foreman a couple of years ago named Cornelius Gentry. But I'm sure it couldn't be the same man."

Kate's concern deepened. "Maybe we should make certain." She came to a decision and shoved back her chair. "Let me run over and ask Lance. If it is the same man, you and your father could be in danger."

Rebecca caught Kate's arm before she could put action to words. "Wait."

Everything inside Rebecca cringed at the notion of confronting Alex again. He and her father had a history. A very volatile history. If Gentry were the man they were after, Alex would find a way to draw her father into the scandal, something she'd do almost anything to avoid.

She leaned across the table and spoke in a low hush. "Kate, what if they want to question me about Gentry? What am I supposed to say to them? I don't have any information about the man other than he's been my father's foreman for the past two years." That, and he gave her the creeps. "Let's wait and get our facts straight. Then we can decide what to do about it. But I'd rather not interrupt them if it isn't Gentry."

Before Kate could respond, Richie arrived with their lunch. Rebecca stared at the beautifully plated food, but found she'd lost her appetite. She could only pray it wasn't her father's foreman. Maybe the name really was Cantry and her imagination was working overtime. That didn't change how she felt about the man. From the moment she'd returned home a year ago and first met him, she'd struggled against her aversion to his presence, trying to impose rationale and logic in the face of her instinctive reaction whenever he came around.

But just that morning she'd had a run-in with him. He'd blocked her exit as she'd been leaving her father's house for the club, standing too close and refusing to move back. In fact, now that she thought about it, it was identical to what had happened between her and Alex. How interesting that with one man she could have melted into his embrace, but with the other, every ounce of intuition had urged her to put as much distance as possible between them.

And he'd sensed how she'd felt. She'd seen it in the narrowing of his hard, brown eyes and the tightening of the fleshy mouth he'd twisted into a grimacing smile. "Miz Becca," he'd greeted her. His gaze had swept over her and his smile had pulled wider. "Don't you look the picture."

"Thanks, Cornelius." She lifted an eyebrow. "If you'll excuse me?"

He'd kept standing there, a knowing look in his eyes, before he'd fallen back a scant step. "Of course, your ladyship. Didn't mean for the hired help to get in your way. Don't want to lose my job the way the Montoyas did. Though it would be a sweet way to go."

Her uncontrollable outrage had only deepened his amusement. "I'm sure my father will be interested in your opinion," she shot back. "I'll be certain to share it with him."

"Feel free. Won't make a lick of difference." He bent

toward her and she couldn't help herself. She turned her head to the side, revealing a vulnerability she'd have preferred to keep hidden. "I'm here to stay, missy. Your father won't dare let me go."

"And then, of course, there's the discrepancy with the club accounts. That's caused an absolute furor among the boys," Kate was saying.

Rebecca came to with a start. "What was that? What discrepancy are you talking about?"

"You haven't listened to a word I've said, have you?" Kate asked in exasperation.

"Most of them." She offered an apologetic smile. "Some of them."

Kate sighed. "Darius noticed discrepancies in the TCC accounts when he did the billing for the Helping Hands women's shelter. Mitch agreed to do a fact-finding audit with Darius, Justin and Alex. Apparently, something's up. At least that's what Lance told me."

"But surely Dad—" She broke off, her nervousness increasing. She cleared her throat. "I wonder why Dad didn't catch the problem? He's been the club treasurer for years."

Kate shrugged. "Maybe it's a recent problem that your father hasn't noticed. It's probably some sort of glitch with funds going into the wrong accounts. I'm sure Mitch will get it straightened out."

Rebecca spared another glance over her shoulder. The six men had disappeared into one of the meeting rooms with the door firmly shut. More than anything she wished she could be a fly on the wall and find out just what the devil was going on. In the meantime, she could only pray her father wasn't unwittingly involved.

It didn't make sense that her father would have anything to do with the fires, but the irregularities of TCC accounts… That might be a different story. Hopefully, it really was a glitch and nothing that would pit her father against her friends. And then there was Alex. He despised her father. If a mistake had been made with the financial records, Alex wouldn't spare him. He'd do anything and everything to ruin her father's reputation.

Alex fixed his gaze on the five men, several of whom had, during his formative years, done their best to make his life a living hell. They stood together in a united front on one side of the room while he planted himself opposite them. Despite the animosity between them, he planned on enjoying the sweetness of his vindication today. Not only would he have the means to bring down an old enemy, but he'd be able to figuratively plant his fist in the face of the worst of the "frat brats" and his key nemesis, Lance Brody.

"Are we going to stand around and stare at each other?" he asked. "Or are we going to start offering apologies?"

"Sure, feel free to apologize, Montoya," Lance said with a grin that didn't come close to reaching his dark eyes. "I've been waiting a lifetime for you to apologize for your existence."

Alex took a swift step in his direction, only to be cut off by Darius who crossed the breach and held up a hand. "Easy man," he said in an undertone. "This won't solve anything."

"Maybe not, but it would make me feel a hell of a lot better."

Alex could hear his accent deepening, thickening, as it often did when he was angry or passionate. It only served to underscore the differences between them—differences in their cultures, their birthrights, their backgrounds. He was the son of a maid. And though some of the men present had worked for every dime they possessed, Justin Dupree and the Brody brothers had been born with silver spoons feeding them every elegant morsel they'd ever eaten. For the sake of his sister, Alicia, Alex would leave her brand new fiancé, Dupree, alone. In the past weeks the two men had established an uneasy accord. But as far as he was concerned, it was open season on the Brodys.

Alex addressed Lance. "You accused me of torching your refinery. Darius has evidence that proves you wrong. Are you man enough to finally admit it? Or do I need to beat the apology out of you?"

Amusement lined the other man's face. "You can try. I guarantee you won't succeed."

"It will be interesting to test that theory."

"Enough." Kevin Novak cut them off impatiently. "This isn't going to solve anything, and quite frankly, I'm tired of acting like we're still in high school." He turned his intense blue eyes on Alex. "We were wrong about you, and I for one would like to apologize."

He offered his hand and Alex didn't hesitate in taking it. "I appreciate it, Novak."

Lance groaned. "Oh, for the love of—"

"Shut up, bro." Mitch cut him off. "A dry well is a dry well. In our business, you have to know when to cut your losses. This is one of those times."

One by one, each man followed Kevin's example. Lance, the lone holdout, finally stepped forward and clasped Alex's hand, as well. Considering Brody was built like a tank, he didn't need to exert much pressure for Alex to feel the power behind his grip.

"I still don't like you," Lance said.

Alex inclined his head. "The feeling's mutual."

Lance's mouth kicked up in one corner. "But I do respect you."

The admission stunned Alex and it took him a second to reply. "I think we can both start from there and see where we end up."

"Fair enough."

"Now that we're through with the warm and fuzzies, let's get to work, shall we?" Darius suggested drily. He made a move toward the conference table and once everyone was seated, passed around copies of his report. "I need everyone here to understand that most of this is speculation. It's solid speculation, but we don't have enough to take to the cops. Yet. The one thing I can state categorically is that Alex is not responsible for the fire at Brody Oil and Gas. I have eyewitnesses and credit card receipts that place him well away from that location on the night of the blaze."

"So, what *do* you have?" Lance asked.

Alex took over. "If we examine the timeline of events, what becomes clear is that there is an interesting order to these incidents. From what Mitch has been able to discover in his review of the books, money has been siphoned off to the tune of three hundred grand."

Kevin emitted a low whistle. "How?"

"Just the way Darius thought. He's been using a company with a name similar to Helping Hands. When an invoice comes in from the shelter, two checks are cut. One to the shelter and a second one to 'Helping Hearts.' Every last one of these checks was cashed at the same bank." Alex eyed each man in turn. "And isn't it interesting that a year ago—right before the first check went through—the president of that bank was approved as a brand-new member of the Texas Cattleman's Club."

"Who put his name forward?" Lance asked.

"Sebastian Huntington."

Lance winced. "Oh, Kate's not going to like this. She and Rebecca are closer than sisters."

"It's our belief," Darius picked up the story, "that Huntington had his foreman, Cornelius Gentry, set the fires in order to pit the six of us against each other to keep us distracted long enough for him to replace the funds. Since he's the treasurer of TCC, he could tidy everything up so that no one was the wiser."

"*If* we'd remained distracted and fighting amongst ourselves," Alex added.

"How did you connect Gentry to the fires?" Justin asked.

Alex eyed his future brother-in-law. "The same way I was let off the hook is the way Gentry was put on it. He drives a pickup similar to mine. And the idiot stopped for gas a mile away from the refinery—fifteen minutes after the place went up in flames."

Darius shook his head in disgusted amusement. "Not the sharpest knife in the drawer, our Gentry." He tapped one of the points in his report. "The police also found identical boot prints at both the refinery blaze, as well as Alex's barn fire. Since they're two sizes smaller than what Alex wears, that's one more piece of evidence that points at someone other than Alex. If we can connect our man to those prints—and I think we can—we'll have something we can use. Connect Gentry to the fires, put some pressure on him, and I think we'll have Huntington."

Lance swore. "I don't like the man, I admit. He's a pompous, arrogant SOB. But even so, he's Rebecca's father and I flat-out adore that woman." He shot Alex a cold look. "Even if she doesn't always show the best judgment in men."

Alex tamped down on the fury sweeping through him. He didn't want to think about Rebecca. Not here, in the presence of these men. He'd thought he could handle seeing Becca again, deal with emotions that shouldn't still be edged with raw pain. But that combined with the animosity that lingered between him and the men in the room with him set his blood boiling. It wasn't just the Brodys' treatment of him during high school and the rivalry he and Lance had experienced on the soccer field. They'd made their disapproval keenly felt when he'd dated Rebecca in college. And when their affair had ended, they'd closed ranks and made his life a living hell.

"Let it go, Lance," Mitch urged.

But he wouldn't, Alex knew. Couldn't. "Say it, Brody," he taunted. "Don't hold back."

Old anger burst free. "You used her. You wanted to screw the daughter of your mother's employer and you did everything and anything necessary to coax her into bed before dumping her like so much garbage. Rumor has it, it was a bet. Is that why you did it? You and your old pal, El Gato, put money on which of you would be the first?"

"You have no idea what you're talking about." The words escaped in a flood of Spanish, but Lance got the gist. "Huntington filled her head with lies—lies she chose to believe."

"That's not the story we heard."

Alex forced himself to relax, using every ounce of the iron will and tenacity that had earned him his first million. He deliberately switched to English. "And we all know how trustworthy Sebastian Huntington is. Clearly, his word is solid."

An uncomfortable silence reigned for a full minute

before Darius tapped the sheaf of papers in front of him. "If we could focus on the matter at hand?" He paused until he had everyone's attention. "The one thing we do have is incontrovertible evidence regarding the embezzlement. And there's little to no doubt Sebastian Huntington is behind it."

"I've spoken with some of the other board members," Mitch offered. "Quietly. Privately. They all say the same thing. They want Huntington to step down as treasurer—"

Justin snorted. "You think?"

"—and replace the money. There's been some talk about his resigning from the club."

"Some *talk?*" Kevin responded indignantly. "You can't be suggesting there's any question about that."

"Apparently there is," Mitch replied. "He's been a member in good standing for decades. We may all consider him a pompous ass, but the old guard is closing ranks."

"Sounds familiar," Alex murmured. He released his breath in a sigh. He didn't know why any of this surprised him, but it did. "I'll speak to Huntington about replacing the money."

The Brody brothers exchanged uneasy glances. "I'm not sure—" Lance began.

Alex cut him off without compunction. "I don't care what you think or what you're sure of or not sure of. *I* will speak to Huntington. Deal with Gentry as you wish. Perhaps you can squeeze the truth out of him. If he points the finger at Rebecca's father, then you may choose how to handle it. I, for one, have no qualms about seeing both Gentry and Huntington locked up for the rest of their miserable lives."

"Regardless of what it'll do to Rebecca?" Lance asked.

Alex leaned across the table toward him, his gaze implacable. "He gave no thought to what it would do to the lives of my mother and sister when he threw us off his ranch. All because I had the temerity to fall in love with his daughter. As far as I'm concerned, my mother's death is a direct result of that man's actions. So, no. I'm not too concerned about Rebecca's feelings when I see to it that her bastard of a father is thrown in jail." He'd had enough. More than enough. He shoved back his chair and stood. "Are we finished here? If so, I have pressing business to attend to."

It was business that would eventually return him to Rebecca's orbit. As he left the meeting room, he glanced toward the café. She was still there, sitting with Kate and picking at her food.

She'd worn her hair up today, piling all that fire and glitter into an elegant little knot on top of her head. Did she have any idea what that hairstyle did to a man? She had a redhead's complexion, her skin the exact shade of rich cream. And her hairstyle exposed the creamy length of her throat and vulnerable nape of her neck to his gaze. When they'd collided earlier, it had taken every bit of control not to feather his fingers along that throat. To restrain from cupping the back of her neck and urging her upward so he could sample her lush mouth and discover if it still tasted as sweet. To watch those witch-green eyes go slumberous with passion.

As much as he despised the woman—as much as Rebecca Huntington had made his life a living hell—he still wanted her. And somehow, someway, he'd have her.

Only this time, it would be on *his* terms.

Two

Rebecca had planned to question her father at dinner that night. But when she entered the dining room, the housekeeper, Louise, informed her that he was dining with his cronies. It seemed ridiculous to eat in solitary splendor, but since the table had been set and the food prepared, there wasn't much she could do except enjoy the lovely meal that had been prepared for her.

Shortly after nine, Louise appeared in the doorway of the library where Rebecca was curled up reading. "There's a visitor to see Mr. Huntington. When I informed him that your father was out for the evening, he insisted on speaking to you."

Alex stepped around Louise and entered the library. "Thank you, I'll take it from here."

Rebecca shot to her feet, her book bouncing onto the floor. Louise stared wide-eyed from one to the other. Clearly, she'd heard the whispers regarding their romantic history and didn't know how to respond. "I'll deal with Mr. Montoya," Rebecca informed the housekeeper.

Alex waited until the door closed behind the woman before bending over and picking up Rebecca's book. He gave the cover a cursory glance before handing it over. "You always did enjoy science fiction."

She didn't bother with the niceties. Instead, she cut straight to business. "Why are you here? Louise said you wanted to speak to Dad."

"Texas Cattleman's Club business. Rather urgent business. Is he really gone, or am I simply *persona non grata?*"

"Both, actually."

He absorbed that with a smile. "When do you expect him?"

Dread gripped her. This must be about the meeting at TCC and the account discrepancy Kate mentioned. Rebecca had called her friend after dinner hoping to get an update, but had been forced to leave a voice mail. Now she wondered if there was a reason Kate elected not to take the call.

She faced Alex with what she hoped was a serene expression. Realizing that he was still waiting for a response, she shrugged. "Dad didn't say when he'd return. Perhaps if you phone him in the morning?"

He laughed. "Get real, Becca. He'd never take the call. I'll wait until he returns. I'm sure you don't mind."

Making himself at home, he removed his suit jacket and dropped it over the back of the nearest chair. His snowy-white shirt stretched across a physique every bit as impressive now as when he'd played soccer. In fact, she found it more impressive with the added heft and refined muscle the years had built into his frame. A silk tie in a deep, rich ruby was knotted at his throat while a gold tie tack and matching cuff links gleamed in the subdued lighting. He was a gorgeous man, fully in his prime. Intelligent. Confident. Wealthy.

And he knew it.

Unless she chose to throw him out—a laughable exercise in futility—she had no option but to surrender gracefully. "What's this about, Alex?" She waved aside the response she knew he'd make. "I know it's TCC business. What, specifically?"

He considered for a moment before inclining his head. "Since I'm sure Kate's already told you, I don't suppose it matters." She didn't bother to correct him, and he continued. "It's regarding an account discrepancy."

She fought to swallow against a throat gone desert dry. "What sort of discrepancy?"

"Some money has gone missing."

Oh, God. "How much?" she asked tightly.

"Three hundred thousand."

The blood drained from her head and she felt her knees buckle. He reached her side before she even sensed him moving. Strong, powerful hands closed around her arms and he ushered her backward the few steps it took to reach the sofa.

"Sit down." When she balked, his voice took on an impatient edge. "Don't be ridiculous, Becca. You're going down whether you sit or fall. Better to sit, yes?"

"You think he stole it, don't you? You think my father's responsible."

He eased her onto the couch cushions and took a seat beside her, his hands still on her. Touching her. Grasping her. Warming her. "I don't *think*." He instantly dashed her hopes by adding, "I *know* he stole the money. The proof is undeniable."

"There must be some mistake, some reasonable explanation—" she began, searching his expression with raw distress. "Please, Alex."

"You always do that." His gaze blistered her, pinning her in place with eyes the color of bitter dark chocolate. "You always defend him. It doesn't matter what he does, how despicable his actions, you always take his side."

"I don't want to discuss our past." She couldn't bear it. Even after seven long years, the hurt was as fresh as yesterday. "He may have fired Carmen, even though I begged him not to, but his actions weren't anywhere near as despicable as your own."

His expression hardened, assuming a ruthlessness she'd never seen in the Alex she'd known all those years ago. "You're talking about the bet."

She attempted to escape the couch, but he held her

in place, refusing to give her the breathing room she needed so desperately. "Of course I'm talking about the bet. The one you made with Rodriquez."

"I've always been curious." He tilted his head to one side while he studied her. "How, precisely, did your father learn of this bet?"

She stirred uncomfortably. "Word gets around, Alex. People…people brag."

"Meaning, I must have bragged, because I was so proud of having won this bet. So, first I coaxed you into my bed on a dare and then I boasted about my success when it proved so easy?" He ignored her flinch. "Yes, I see that's what you believe. Because that was the sort of man I was. A man who steals innocence and brags of his misdeeds. A man who lies and cheats to get what he wants."

"Don't do this, Alejandro."

But he didn't relent. "And because I was this liar, this cheat, this ruiner of all pure and wholesome, your father lashed out at—not just me—but my family, as well. As payback for having the audacity to touch you, he left my sister homeless and caused my mother to work herself into an early grave. This is the man you defend, *dulzura?*"

She would have covered her ears if she could have. But he continued to hold her, forcing her to hear each hideous word. "Don't. Don't call me that. You don't have the right. Not any longer."

It was the wrong thing to say. "I've never had the right, have I?" he demanded in a harsh voice. "Even though you took me into your bed, you still felt guilty. Tarnished."

"That's not true," she instantly denied. "I loved you."

"The housekeeper's son."

How could he think such a thing? She'd never felt that way. Never. "I didn't care. It didn't matter."

His eyes blazed. "You mean it doesn't matter *now*. Now that I have money and status and a ranch that rivals any in Maverick County." With a muttered curse, he ripped at the knot anchoring his tie as though it were strangling him, and removed the gold tie tack. Up close, she realized it was a beautifully scripted *M*. He slipped it into his pocket before leaning in. "And now I have the power to determine your father's future…as well as your own."

None of this made sense. Not any of it. "My father is renowned for his investment acumen. His business abilities are unparalleled. Why in the world would he need to embezzle money from the club?" Rebecca demanded. "Obviously, there's been some sort of mistake."

"You're right. There has. And your father made it. Even worse, he made it right in front of me, where I could have the pleasure of playing sheriff to his bank robber."

She moistened her lips while she struggled to find some answer to his accusation. In response, a flame of desire licked across his expression. Just like that, time slowed and her world tipped in a new and dangerous direction. It was as though all her senses grew more acute and intensely focused, consumed by her reaction to one man.

Alejandro Montoya.

Sound dampened. The only whisper slipping through was the labored give and take of their breath. She inhaled sharply, but all that did was fill her lungs with his unique scent, something crisp and spicy. Exotic. His hands tightened on her arms and she remembered how they'd felt against her skin all those years ago. Strong, when they swept her up and carried her to his bed. Tender, when he'd undressed her and caressed parts of her no man had seen or touched until that moment. Gentle, when he'd mated his body to hers and taught her a passion she'd only dreamed about.

Rebecca's surroundings melted and all she could see was Alex. He became her universe. He leaned in, so slowly she couldn't mistake his intent. So slowly, that she could have avoided the embrace if she'd truly wanted to. She didn't. She wished she could have claimed it was simple curiosity. But it went far beyond that. She needed to know, once and for all, whether the heat between them was real, or mere shadows of what they'd once shared.

"Dulzura…" he murmured.

And then he consumed her. How could she have forgotten how it had been between them? Or perhaps she hadn't forgotten. Living without him and what he'd given her had been too painful to bear, so she'd pushed the memories from her mind as an act of self-protection. Now those memories came crashing down, ripping her apart like shards of broken glass.

His mouth shifted over hers, firm and experienced,

with more assurance than ever. Where before he'd coax her lips apart, this time he demanded. She didn't want to resist, it seemed so pointless. So she didn't. Her mouth parted beneath his and she shuddered in the taking, the clever parry of tongue and nip of teeth, combined with the sweet, sweet flavor of him.

The sofa cushions caught her as Rebecca fell backward. Alex followed her down, settling angles over the soft give of her body, angles that had grown sharper and more defined with the passage of the years. While his hands coasted along her sides and swept upward beneath the flowing cotton blouse she wore, hers made short work of the buttons hindering her own path. At long last, she yanked apart the edges of his shirt and found the warmth beneath, reacquainting herself with every muscular knot and burl.

He followed suit and she shuddered at the sweep of the calloused ridges of his fingers and palms. He might be one of the wealthiest businessmen in the state, but at heart he was, and always would be, one with the land. El Diablo wasn't just a rich man's toy. It was a working ranch, and based on the calluses on his hands and the lean, sculpted expanse beneath her fingers, he worked it himself.

His hands stroked upward until they closed over her unfettered breasts, cupping the weight of them in his palms. "I could never get over the softness of your skin. It feels like velvet. But when I look at it…I swear, it's paler than moonbeams."

His thumbs drifted across the tips of her breasts in a tantalizing circle and the softest of moans escaped her. She couldn't help herself. She cupped his face, tracing the elegant contours. Sweeping cheekbones above shallow hollows. A wide mouth that begged to be kissed, framed by deep brackets of painful experience. A squared jaw with just the shadow of an indent, one she'd traced with her index finger on countless occasions.

She slid her hands into his hair to anchor him in place, taking private delight in gaining control of the embrace. Lifting upward, she nibbled at his lips, teasing at them until he groaned and sank back against her. She parted her legs to give him more room, running her bare foot along his calf, secretly amused as she pressed a series of wrinkles into the crisp material of his trouser leg. She wanted to take the urbane businessman and strip away the outer layer of sophistication, to reduce him to that elemental core that made him so unique and distinctive. To find again the pure masculine essence of the man she'd fallen in love with.

It was a moment out of time. A moment of indulgence. A moment that came to a shocking end when the door to the library slammed open against the wall.

"What the *hell* is going on?" Sebastian Huntington demanded.

Her father's arrival snapped her out of her sensual haze as effectively as a hypnotist snapping his subject out of a trance. She knew there was no point in trying to shove Alex off her. For one thing, he was far too heavy and strong, particularly if he had no intention of getting off—which she suspected was true in this case. Plus, the damage had been done.

Alex glanced across the room at her father and bared his teeth in a wolfish smile. "You're interrupting a private moment," he said. "Next time, you might consider knocking before you barge in."

Sebastian stared, stunned. "It…it's *my* house," he sputtered in protest. "I don't have to knock to enter a room in my own house."

"You do if you want to avoid scenes like this." Alex levered himself off Rebecca and shoved his hands through the hair she'd taken such delight in rumpling. Then he held out his hand and helped her escape the embrace of the sofa cushions. He took his time buttoning his shirt and tucking it into his trousers. He didn't bother to adjust his tie, but left it dangling. "I see you're still as arrogant as ever, Huntington. Let's see how long that lasts."

"Alex," Rebecca attempted to intercede.

He simply shook his head. "This doesn't involve you, Becca."

"But—"

He shot her a single look and she fell silent. Unfortunately, he was right. This was none of her business, other than the fact that her father was somehow involved. She wasn't privy to whatever information he had about the missing money, or what mistakes might have occurred that led Alex to believe her father had committed the crime. But she could stand beside her father and support him while he cleared up the misunderstanding.

"What are you doing here?" Sebastian demanded. He shot Rebecca a look of intense rebuke. "Other than attacking my daughter."

"Is that how it looked to you?" A genuine grin broke across Alex's face. "Well, whatever allows you to sleep at night."

Dull color crept up the older man's cheekbones. "I repeat. Why are you here?"

"I've been asked to come. The board of the TCC requested it."

To Rebecca's horror, every scrap of color drained from her father's face. His jaw worked for a moment before he managed to say, "I don't believe you."

"Discrepancies have been discovered in the club's financial accounts. Checks have been paid out to at least one bogus company." His mouth took on a taunting slant. "Checks you endorsed."

Sebastian's hands clenched into fists. "The only checks I've written have been in response to legitimate billing statements."

Alex folded his arms across his chest. "Like to Helping Hearts?"

Rebecca frowned. "Don't you mean Helping Hands?" she asked. "That's the women's shelter where Summer works. Aren't they part of an outreach program that the Texas Cattleman's Club funds?"

"Helping *Hands* is the outreach program we assist. I

couldn't tell you what Helping Hearts is," Alex replied. Though he addressed Rebecca, his gaze remained fixed on Sebastian. "But since your father cut several generous checks to them, I'm hoping he can tell me. Especially considering all of them were cashed at the same bank by none other than the president of that fine, upstanding institution—who, coincidentally enough, joined TCC shortly before the first check was cashed." He allowed that information to sink in. "So explain it to your daughter, Sebastian. What exactly is Helping Hearts?"

To Rebecca's shock, beads of sweat broke out across her father's forehead. "I'd have to check the records, examine the invoices, assuming they can be found."

"That's easy enough. I have a copy of the checks in question, all signed by you and approved by your banker friend, Rhymes. But the invoices are conveniently missing."

Sebastian's chin lifted. "Then I don't see how I can help you."

"All of the invoices for Helping Hearts are missing," Alex repeated softly. "Quite a coincidence, wouldn't you say?"

"It happens. They were probably misfiled."

"Or shredded, assuming they ever existed."

Sebastian shrugged. "If that's all…?"

"Not even close. There's going to be an audit, Huntington. And when it's done, you will be, as well. How much will they find missing? From what little we've been able to dig up, it's in the neighborhood of three hundred grand."

"Dad!"

Sebastian flinched. "You have no right—"

Alex stepped forward, his voice low and hard. "We have every right, you son of a bitch. You sit in your fine mansion and act as though you're somehow superior to everyone else."

"I can trace my birthright back to—"

Alex cut him off. "Who cares? You think that will matter to the board? Save it for your cellmates. Maybe they'll give a damn who your ancestors were and what they accomplished. Personally, I don't see a pedigree when I look at you. All I see is a thief."

Sebastian pulled at his tie as though it were choking him. "You have no proof!"

"How long do you think it'll take for me to get it? Do you think Rhymes will stand by you when we trace those checks back to him and accuse him of fraud? Where do you think he'll point the finger, especially if he's offered a deal?" Sebastian's breath quickened and he wiped his brow with a hand that trembled, but it was clear that Alex wasn't finished. "Just like Gentry is going to point the finger at you as the instigator when we pin him for torching Brody Oil and Gas and my barn."

"What?"

Sebastian stumbled and Rebecca darted to his side, helping him to the nearest chair. Then she hurried across the room and splashed a generous finger of whiskey into a tumbler. Returning to her father's side, she pressed the glass into his hands.

"Easy, Dad. Drink this."

"I swear to you, Rebecca," he said in an undertone. "I had nothing to do with those fires. I have no idea what Montoya is talking about."

She believed him. "Why would my father ask his foreman to set those fires?" she demanded of Alex. "What possible motive could he have?"

"We wondered the same thing," he admitted. "But considering how everyone's been running around like a bunch of crazed ants when their anthill has been kicked over, the motive became clear enough. Your father needed to keep the Brodys, me and several other key members of the TCC too busy to look at the accounts. To keep us fighting among ourselves while he covered his tracks."

"You're insane," Sebastian whispered. Then his eyes widened. "My God! You think I don't see what's going on here? You're behind the arson fires—assuming it really was arson."

Alex laughed in genuine amusement. "Why would I burn my own barn?"

"To implicate me." Her father's voice grew more assertive. "You're a fool, Montoya, if you think anyone will believe me capable of such an act. They'll all see this for what it really is—your petty stab at revenge for my having fired your mother all those years ago. I had nothing to do with those fires. Nothing."

She couldn't help but notice that he didn't deny dipping into TCC funds and her heart sank. "The money?" she asked tentatively.

He tossed back the whiskey, then closed his eyes and nodded his head. For a full thirty seconds, she couldn't move. Couldn't seem to process the truth. Then it all came crashing down on her. No. Oh, please, no. How could her father have done such a thing? *Why* would he?

Aware of Alex's intent gaze, she slowly straightened and faced him. "If—and I stress the word *if*—my father did contribute to some sort of accounting error—"

"So gently put." Alex's expression hardened. "It's called embezzlement, Becca. He stole the money."

She pressed her lips together to keep them from betraying her panic. "If he stole the money, will you give him an opportunity to return it?"

"I don't have it," Sebastian said wearily. "I invested it and the investment hasn't come through yet."

A small cry of distress escaped, despite her best efforts to control it. "Why? Why would you do such a thing?"

"Because he's arrogant." Alex answered the question before Sebastian had the opportunity. "Because he feels he's entitled."

"Because I'm on the verge of bankruptcy and thought this investment would turn everything around. Rodriquez swore it would."

Rebecca could literally feel the change in the atmosphere, the way it stilled and thickened. "Rodriquez?" Alex repeated. "Paulo?"

Sebastian shrugged. "Paulo. El Gato. Your old friend from the barrio. I didn't realize he was behind the investment opportunities until it was too late to pull out.

The first few ventures went well enough. We both made a modest amount of money. But then, it all went to hell. I realized I was in far deeper than I'd planned."

"How?" Alex demanded.

"He offered to let me pay a mere pittance of my actual stake, and foolishly I went along. When the deal went south, I had to come up with the balance of the money, fast. That's when I found out the identity of my new partner." He gave Alex a pained look. "I don't have to tell you that Rodriquez plays for keeps."

"So you stole the money from TCC."

"Yes. The plan was to replace it as soon as I received my return on our final investment."

"Only it didn't work out quite that way. That investment went sour, as well."

Sebastian's mouth twisted. "I see you know how it works. I should have figured it out long before I did and cut my losses. Instead, I borrowed—"

"Stole," Alex cut in.

Sebastian's head jerked up and he glared across the room. "You want your pound of flesh, don't you, boy?"

Alex took a single step in Sebastian's direction, but it was enough to make the older man shrink into his chair. "First, Huntington, I'm no longer a boy. I haven't been since the day you destroyed my family."

"You destroyed them yourself!" Sebastian fought back. "If you'd kept your hands off my daughter, none of this would have happened."

Alex continued as though he'd never been interrupted. "And second, you're right. I intend to have my pound of flesh. Every last ounce of it. I appreciate your making it so easy for me."

Sebastian rose to his feet, trembling with the effort. "Fine. I *stole.* Does that make you happy? I stole money from TCC and gave it to Rodriquez. He swore this last deal would finish the matter between us." He laughed without humor. "He was right. It has. I have no more money to give him—hell, I still owe him a bloody fortune—and I don't doubt that I'll soon hear that our investment met with tragic results."

"Count on it." Alex folded his arms across his chest. "So, if you're on the verge of bankruptcy, how do you plan to pay back the money?" He glanced around. "I suppose you could always sell your home, and the land that's been in your family for countless generations. Move to more modest accommodations."

A hideous silence settled over them, one that Rebecca finally broke. "I'll sell Sweet Nothings," she said quietly. "I own the building, as well as the business. There should be more than enough to cover what my father owes the club, and possibly El Gato, too."

"No," Sebastian and Alex said in unison.

If circumstances had been different, she'd have smiled at their unusual accord. But right now, she didn't find anything about the situation even remotely amusing. "Neither of you has any say in this."

"That's where you're wrong," Alex corrected her. "This is your father's debt and he'll pay it, not you."

"You can't stop me, Alex," she argued. "If I choose to liquidate Sweet Nothings, that's my business."

"And when word gets out about the reason for liquidating your shop?" Alex shot back. "Somerset's a small town. Do you really think your father will be able to hold his head up when everyone learns that he's a thief? That he allowed his daughter to bail him out? It won't be long before he sells, if only because he can no longer handle the whispers and looks of disgust. The sheer humiliation of it all. Who will welcome the Huntingtons into their homes?" He allowed that to sink in. "No one. You will be outcasts."

"You have a better suggestion?" Rebecca demanded.

"He sells his homestead to me. The money is replaced quietly, with no scandal. I'll handle Rodriquez. And then your father leaves Maverick County. I'll see to it that he has sufficient funds to keep him in comfort for the rest of his days—assuming he's careful and doesn't make any more risky business ventures. But Huntington Manor will become Montoya property from this point forward."

Three

"Get out!" Sebastian snarled. "Get out of my home, you vulture. I'll find my own solution to this mess. This land will never bear your name. Never, do you hear me?"

Alex just smiled. "You have three days to return the money to TCC or the board will be contacting the authorities. They've also relieved you as treasurer and appointed Mitch Brody in your place. Consider your membership officially suspended." He picked up his suit jacket from the back of the chair where he'd left it and shrugged it on. "I'll see myself out."

Rebecca spared a brief, anguished glance at her father, and followed Alex. She caught up with him in the foyer. "Wait."

He paused by the front door and turned to confront her. "You'd be wise to stay out of this, Rebecca."

So formal. So cold. Even so, she couldn't let him go. Not without doing everything within her power to stop events from moving any further along this path of destruction. It didn't matter if she had to swallow every last ounce of pride. If it meant a quiet and reasonable solution to her father's dilemma, she'd do it. "Please, Alex. There must be another way of resolving this."

He turned on her. "I've never met a woman who possesses even a tenth of the loyalty you display toward your father," he marveled. "It doesn't matter what he does to you, to the people dependent on him for a living, to casual bystanders who get in his way. You still defend him."

She shook her head in instant denial. "I'm not defending him. If he stole the money—"

Alex lifted an eyebrow. "If?" he repeated softly.

She hovered between crazed laughter and tears. "I know he stole the money." The wound was so new and raw, she couldn't even fully feel the hurt. But she didn't doubt for a minute that would change. And soon. "I guess I haven't digested it yet."

"I suggest you start. As of tomorrow, your life will take a dramatic change."

"My life?" She stared at him, not understanding. "It's my father—"

He simply shook his head. "You've lived in Somerset all your life and still you don't know how things work?"

he said with disbelief. "How many of your so-called friends will stand beside you when it's discovered that your father is a thief?"

It took her an instant to comprehend his words. "But they're my friends," she replied. "Why wouldn't they—"

He gave a short, hard laugh. "Grow up, Becca. Your father is already teetering on the edge of bankruptcy. He earns—earned—his living investing other people's money. Who do you think will invest their money with him after this? Do you think they won't wonder whether he somehow scammed them during one of their past associations? That they won't make accusations, if only to one another?"

A denial leaped to her lips, one she didn't dare utter. Until today she'd have sworn her father was as honest as the day was long, that his pride in his name and reputation and family honor meant everything to him. But she didn't know the man sitting in their library, a man who had confessed to a crime that her father had always taught her ranked just shy of murder.

"I see you're starting to understand," Alex said. "It's time to face facts, Rebecca. Your life as you knew it is over. Who will want anything to do with you or your father? Maybe his dishonesty is a genetic trait. Maybe you were in on it. And how delighted some will be that the mighty Huntingtons have finally gotten their—" He tilted his head to one side in consideration. "What is that antiquated phrase? Ah, yes. Comeuppance."

"Is that how you see us, Alex?" She dared to close the distance between them. "Is that how you see me? As the daughter of a thief?"

"It's what you are." He spoke the words—brutal, unkind words. They'd have wounded her beyond bearing if she hadn't seen the truth on his face. He didn't believe those words. Not even a little. Regret already glittered in the inky depths of his eyes. "Becca—"

"Tell me what we can do. Tell me what you want."

The regret vanished as if it had never been. "And you'll give it to me?"

"Yes. Ask and it's yours."

"Just to make all this go away?"

Her chin shot up. "Not go away. My father owes the money. If it takes us the rest of our lives, it'll be repaid. If it can be done quietly, fine. If it can't, it will still be repaid." She stepped even closer. "But he's not responsible for those arson fires. I'll never believe it."

"Yesterday, you'd never have believed your father was a thief."

"Help me, Alex." She couldn't believe she was asking, but what choice did she have? Once Alex set himself a course, he wouldn't be dissuaded. If she could focus that determination on his finding the true culprit for the arson fires, it would prove her father's innocence. "I'm only asking you to help me find the truth. Help me find out who's really responsible for setting the fires at the refinery and at your ranch."

"And in exchange, you'll give me whatever I want?"

"Yes."

He hooked a finger in the neckline of her cotton blouse and tugged her closer. "What if it's you I want, *dulzura?* How far will you go, and how much will you give me, if I make you the price for my help?"

She didn't hesitate. "All I want is the same thing you do. The truth. And I'll go as far as you want and give whatever you ask in order to get that truth."

"I was hoping you'd say that."

He cupped the back of her neck and took her mouth in a kiss that threatened to destroy what little sanity she retained. His mouth didn't just take hers, it possessed it, consumed it, set her on fire and then drove those flames into an inferno. And then he released her and stepped back. A late fall chill swept in, replacing the warmth from his embrace.

"You tempt me, *dulzura.*" He fixed her with an unreadable gaze. "Unfortunately for you, I'm not a man so easily bought."

And with that, he left her standing in the foyer, utterly devastated.

Rebecca gave herself a day. One single day to get her head straight, her heart protected, and her determination to a point where it outweighed her desperation, before confronting Alex again.

She wished it could be on her territory, or at the very least at a neutral site, but he made that impossible. He didn't show up at the Cattleman's Club, nor at work where she might catch him on the fly. Instead, she was forced to drive out to his ranch, El Diablo.

At the entryway to his gravel drive, she pulled her convertible to the shoulder of the road and climbed out of the car to gaze at his spread. It was an impressive place, rolling across a full hundred acres of windswept pastureland. The ranch house occupied the southeast corner of his property and from her viewpoint she could see several fenced paddocks and a large barn, which was currently under construction. The general noise of that construction drifted toward her, the sound of saws and hammers and the occasional shout borne to her on the chilly fall breeze.

The mansion—for it could hardly be called a house—stood crisp and white against a cerulean sky, the central portion a stately two stories, complete with porticos and balconies, while the sides sprawled outward in wide-flung wings like a warm Texan embrace. The sight filled her with dismay.

Seeing El Diablo in all its glory proved once and for all that this wasn't *her* Alex anymore. She'd known that. Known it for a very long time. But until this minute, she hadn't fully allowed herself to see him as the man he'd become, versus the younger, slightly less powerful version he'd been when they'd first fallen in love. Alejandro Montoya wasn't a poor teen from the barrio anymore. He was a male at his full strength and capability, a force to be reckoned with. He was also a rich, successful, influential man intent on destroying her father.

Rebecca's mouth firmed and she set her chin at a defiant angle. Forewarned was forearmed. Somehow, someway, she would get through to him and resolve this situation, to their mutual advantage.

Returning to the car, she drove down the sweeping drive and parked a short distance from the barn, where she suspected she'd find him. Sure enough, he stood near the main entrance, blueprints spread across a table made from plywood and supported by a pair of saw-horses. A hammer, a crowbar and a can of nails kept the sheets of paper from rolling up.

"We need the rough on the plumbing completed today, as well as the electrical," Alex was saying. "Make sure he puts bibs here, here and here. The building in-spector comes tomorrow and I won't be pleased if there are any delays. Winter's not that far off and I want this place finished before Christmas."

"Yessir, Mr. Montoya. That won't be a problem."

"Thanks, Hank." He looked up then, his gaze sharp and direct beneath the brim of his Stetson. He didn't appear surprised to see her. No doubt he'd been expect-ing this visit. "I'm honored."

Okay, color her surprised. "And why is that?"

"For the first time since I've taken ownership of El Diablo, a Huntington has come to call."

"And yet, no brass band or groveling peasants," she dared to tease.

His mouth twitched before he regained control with characteristic ruthlessness. "I won't bother to ask why you're here. I'll just tell you that you're wasting both your time and mine. You may have endless hours to fritter away. I don't."

"But you'll listen to my pitch, anyway."

He lifted an eyebrow at her confident retort, then jerked his head at Hank. The construction foreman took the hint and made himself scarce.

"Pitch away," Alex instructed. She'd never seen him look harder or more remote. A wall of granite would offer a softer embrace than this man. "Not that it'll do you any good. I have your father right where I want him and nothing you do or say is going to make a bit of difference. So you go right ahead, Ms. Huntington. Lob your best pitch."

She struggled to conceal her dismay. "Here?"

"I'm a busy man. And this has already taken more time than I can spare." He tugged off his leather work gloves and slapped them onto the makeshift table. Planting his palms on the rough wood, he leaned in her direction, the sheer, unadulterated essence of the man threatening to swamp her senses. "So it's here and now, or not at all."

"Okay, fine." She took a deep breath. "I'm asking you…begging you…to help me find out who started those fires. To find out who's really behind them. I know you think it's my father, but I'm telling you, it's not. He's guilty of—" She forced herself to say the words, no matter how acrid they tasted. "He's guilty of theft. But not arson."

Alex simply shook his head. "It's not my job to find who started the blazes."

She marshaled her arguments. "When you put your mind to something, you do it. You make things happen. Please, make this happen."

He was shaking his head again before she'd even finished. "There is nothing you can say, nothing you can offer, no inducement tempting enough for me to assist you or your father in this matter. Stay out of it before he takes you down, too."

She could see the strength of his decision in his set expression and the burning coldness of his gaze. Time to try a different tack. "We also need to talk about the repayment of the money owed to the TCC."

Even on this point he remained unrelenting. "That's between your father and the club."

Alex may have temporarily won their first round, but he wouldn't win this one. When it came to stubborn, she was his equal. "If we could just have a little time," she began. "I could make payments—"

"Forget it, Becca," he interrupted curtly. "Do you think the Texas Cattleman's Club is going to wait years for you and your father to pay back the money he stole? They're barely willing to wait days. If it had been left up to Brody, your father would be cooling his heels in a jail cell as we speak."

He couldn't have shocked her more if he'd slapped her. "Brody? Lance Brody? Kate's Lance?"

He didn't spare her. "That's right. Once he was in possession of all the details, your best friend's husband demanded that the board have your father arrested. But the board decided to give him the chance to repay the money. My offer to purchase Huntington Manor was his one shot at doing just that."

That stung. "I'd be far more appreciative if I didn't know that your motivation for doing so was to get your hands on our home," she shot back.

"Get my hands—" He broke off with a word that had color warming her cheeks. "Why the hell would I want Huntington Manor when I have El Diablo? Your home is a financial sinkhole. Who could afford to buy it, let alone maintain it?"

That shook her and she scrambled for understanding. "You want revenge. You want to drive my father out of Maverick County."

He didn't deny it. "I would prefer to do both of those things without having such an albatross hanging around my neck. Look around you, Becca. El Diablo is a working ranch. My import/export business doesn't carry this place. Far from it. I work hard to keep the ranch solidly in the black. Your father, on the other hand, plays at being a rancher. But I guarantee it doesn't turn a profit and hasn't for a long time."

"I don't understand. Then why…?"

"Why would I offer to buy Huntington Manor so your father can pay off the debt? Simple. I want him gone. He doesn't realize it, yet, but he's out of options. Either he sells to me or he sells to Rodriquez. But he will have to sell out. And soon."

"Rodriquez." Something her father had said the

previous night gnawed at the back of her mind. "Dad says he owes him money, too."

Alex nodded. "I'm sure it's more than either you or your father can get your hands on."

"But if you loaned us the money using Sweet Nothings as collateral, that would be enough, wouldn't it?"

He shrugged. "This isn't my problem, Rebecca. Don't put me in the middle of it."

"You came to us as the Cattleman's representative, remember?" she retorted. "You put yourself in the middle."

"It's out of my hands. Mitch Brody has taken over as club accountant. Talk to him."

"I already did. He needs the cash and we don't have it. But I do have this." She opened her purse and removed the deed to Sweet Nothings and centered it on the plywood between his widespread hands. "As I told you last night, I own both the building, as well as the business. Combined, they're worth well in excess of what Dad owes the TCC."

He made no move to pick up the deed. "We've already discussed this."

"We're discussing it again," she stated evenly. "I can't approach Rhymes for a bank loan using the property as collateral, since he's involved in whatever my father pulled. So, I'm asking you. Will you draw up a loan agreement using Sweet Nothings as collateral?"

He didn't even hesitate. "No. Ask the Brodys. They're your friends, not me."

"That's precisely why I can't ask them," she argued.

"They're friends. It would put them in an awkward position and I refuse to do that to them. But if you loan me the money, everyone will know it's on the up and up because you despise my father."

A humorless laugh stirred the air between them. "I have never understood your brand of logic, and I doubt I ever will." He rocked backward and thought for a moment. "Okay, I'll bite. How will the good people of Maverick county know it's on the up and up? I seem to recall we have a romantic history between us."

"A history that didn't end well," she pointed out. "You have every reason *not* to help us and damn few reasons to go along with this."

"Precisely."

He allowed the word to linger until she released a sigh. "I have two goals, Alex. The first is to help my father repay the money he owes. I guarantee *someone* will loan me the money. My second goal is to prove that my father is innocent of the arson fires and find the person who's actually guilty."

"Not a wise move, Becca. In fact, it's a downright dangerous one."

"Really? There's a way you can stop me." She tapped the deed. "Accept my offer and go with me to visit Darius so he can explain why he thinks my father is complicit in these fires. Help me figure out the identity of the guilty party. Otherwise, I'm taking my offer elsewhere."

His mouth carved into a cynical smile. "I thought you weren't going to approach your friends."

"I'm not. But since El Gato has a vested interest in all this, perhaps he'll be willing to help me."

"Absolutely not!" Alex bit out.

She could tell that the words escaped before he'd had time to think better of them, or he'd never have given her so much leverage in their little skirmish. She offered him a gentle smile and waited. It didn't take long. He snatched off his hat, flung it into the dirt at his feet and swore. She suspected that if he'd cursed in English, she'd have been quite shocked.

"I take it that means you agree?" she dared to ask.

He shot her a black glare. "Let me make myself clear, Rebecca. You are not going to ask Paulo Rodriquez for anything, particularly not a loan."

Interesting. She tilted her head to one side. "I don't understand. I thought he was your friend."

"He was. Is. We grew up together, were close childhood friends. Until recent events, I'd have said we were still friends. But since it was Paulo who helped put your father in his current predicament, you'd be wise to stay well away from him."

She didn't disagree. In fact, she'd deliberately used the name just to goad him. Now he'd roused her curiosity. "Why shouldn't I approach El Gato?"

His mouth tightened, a clear warning signal. "Because I don't know what he wants from your father. Until I do, it isn't safe for you to put yourself between them. And it sure as hell isn't wise to give Rodriquez leverage over you." His gaze swept over her, the sensation almost as tantalizing as a touch. To her dismay it elicited the same reaction, a deep welling of heat and desire, one it took every ounce of willpower to conceal from his discerning eyes. "Nor should you give me that sort of leverage."

"Just out of curiosity, would you use it to hurt me?" She couldn't resist the question, any more than she could deny her interest in his response.

"I'd rather not find out." He bent to pick up his hat, the set of his face making it clear he'd reached a decision. "I'll take you to see Darius. Maybe he can talk some sense into you. At the very least he can give you a general idea why we think your father is behind the arson fires."

"This isn't just about your vendetta against my father, is it?" she asked in dismay. "You really believe he's guilty, don't you?"

He didn't hesitate. "I don't doubt for an instant that he's guilty as sin."

After taking a few minutes to give instructions to Hank, followed by a call to Darius, eliciting the information that the security consultant was at the club, Alex gestured toward her car. "Shall we go together or separately?"

"Together," she decided.

That way she'd have time to further discuss the situation with him—or rather, argue. And if she were brutally honest with herself, she'd also admit that arriving together at the club as a couple would be far less traumatic than enduring the potential stares and whispers from the members if she arrived on her own. The uncomfortable thought gave rise to an even more uncomfortable re- alization.

She waited until they were clear of his drive before asking a question that left her feeling equally embar- rassed and ashamed. "When Dad resigns, the board will want my resignation, too, won't they?"

Alex hesitated before replying. "I don't see why they would."

"You know why," she whispered, not daring to look his way.

"We'll worry about it if it happens."

We. That single word gave her hope. He wasn't to- tally immune to her or to what she was going through. Maybe she could convince him to help her, to get to the truth. If that proof led to her father, so be it. But she was certain, with every fiber of her being, that as guilty as her father was of embezzlement, he was innocent of arson.

The fact that his fate rested in the hands of men who would just as soon see Sebastian Huntington in jail as get at that truth, couldn't be taken lightly. But some- how, someway, she'd find a means to convince them to put aside their animosity and find the actual person responsible.

Nervous dread swept over her as they approached the entryway to the club. "What is Darius going to tell me?" she asked as calmly as she could manage.

"That your father is guilty."

She gave him a brief, searching glance. "I'm serious, Alex. What incontrovertible proof has Darius found?"

"He isn't going to share that with you, Becca."

"Why not?" she demanded.

"Because it would undermine the D.A.'s legal efforts to prosecute your father." He shifted in the leather seat, angling so he could look at her. "Fair warning. There isn't going to be any plea bargaining this down. When we get all the evidence we need, the guilty party is going to jail. End of story."

She understood on an intellectual level that Alex had good cause to feel that way. But this was her father, the man who'd loved and protected her, who'd comforted her when her mother had died. The man who'd raised her and taught her right from wrong. Tears pricked her eyes as she acknowledged his flaws, the incredible distance he'd stepped over the line between honesty and dishonesty, a line he'd once taught her was intransigent.

She refused to believe he'd fallen so far that he'd put the lives of men and livestock, who could have been injured by the blaze at El Diablo, in jeopardy. Parking the car beneath the shade of a wide-flung cottonwood tree she drew in a deep breath, fighting to find some sort of balance amidst the emotional seesaw she'd been on the past forty-eight hours. Was it only two days ago that she'd arrived here to have lunch with Kate? It seemed like an eternity.

"Are you ready?"

The sheer gentleness of the question nearly proved

her undoing. Tears flooded her eyes, tears she suppressed with single-minded determination. She kept her gaze fixed straight ahead while she struggled for control. She needed to put her emotions aside and remain focused on her goals. Otherwise, she'd fall apart and there would be no one left willing to lift a finger to keep her father out of jail. She snatched another quick breath and that's when she felt it.

It was the lightest of touches. Just a fleeting caress along the curve of her cheek. Memories swamped her at the familiar gesture. How many times in the past had Alex comforted her in just that way, lifted her during difficult times with a simple reassuring stroke of his hand? The fact that he'd offer it now, when they were so at odds, meant more than she could ever express.

Energy and sheer obstinacy flowed through her, lending her the strength she so desperately needed. Her chin firmed and she turned toward him, every scrap of grit and purpose concentrated on the goal at hand. "I'm ready," she told him. "I want to know just what we're up against."

She could see his conflicted response to her comment. Part of him—no doubt a reluctant part—wanted to reassure her, while the other intended her to understand the futility of her hopes. He blew out his breath in a sigh. "I'm afraid you're in for a world of disappointment."

"Let's find out."

To her dismay, his words proved prophetic. Darius didn't have any particular ax to grind. His approach was simple: What evidence had he uncovered, and what possible conclusions did that evidence allow him to draw? He took her through it with matter-of-fact precision, his attitude professional, logical, but with an edge of compassion that caused Rebecca to realize that Summer Martindale had chosen wisely when she'd eloped with Darius.

The proof he'd compiled against Cornelius Gentry was formidable. Even so, it wasn't direct or even circumstantial proof against Sebastian Huntington, as she was quick to point out. Gentry could have been acting on his own.

"That's possible," Darius conceded. "Though considering the nature of the man, it's unlikely. Until he's found, we won't know for certain."

"He's disappeared?" Rebecca asked in concern.

Alex didn't bother to hide his cynicism. "Most likely, he was paid to disappear."

She rounded on him. "And you believe my father paid him?"

"It would be in his best interest."

"That doesn't make sense." She'd gotten their attention with that simple statement. A twinge of hope stirred, along with a hint of relief. The more she considered it, the more certain she grew. "I'm serious. Think about it. My father, in effect, gambled away TCC funds by investing them with Paulo Rodriquez, right?"

Both men nodded.

"If he'd had any spare money, he'd have repaid the

club so he wouldn't get caught and accused of embezzlement. So where did he find the money to make
Gentry disappear? I know the man." She couldn't
conceal her shiver of dislike. "He would require some
serious money to go away."

"What do you mean you know him?" Alex asked
sharply.

She hesitated before admitting, "I've had a few run-
ins with him." Both men fixed her with identical looks,
and she caved beneath the joint pressure. "He was too
familiar. Cocky. Arrogant. And when I gave him a verbal
slap, he laughed at me. He told me my father would
never fire him."

Darius groaned. "That doesn't help build a case for
your father's innocence, Rebecca."

"The reverse, in fact," Alex added.

"What? Why?" she asked in alarm.

"Your father destroyed my family when I dared to
touch you. I assume Gentry knew what your father had
done to us?" Alex asked with surprising compassion.

She moistened her lips. "He knew. He said my father
would never fire him the way he had Carmen."

The touch of pity in Alex's gaze totally unnerved
her. "If Gentry was that certain of his position, he must
have had something on your father. Something serious.
If he set the blazes at your father's instruction, he'd
have reason for that sort of confidence."

Four

It took Rebecca a moment to absorb Alex's comment. The instant she did, her breath caught in a gasp.

"No." She shook her head, adamant. "No, that can't be it. Gentry must have known about the money. Thought he could use that as leverage."

"How?" Alex persisted. "It's not likely your father would have mentioned it to him."

"Maybe he overheard a phone conversation between my father and Rhymes." She could hear the desperation in her voice. "There could be any number of ways Gentry could have gotten hold of the information. Besides, what possible motivation could my father have for setting fire to Brody Oil and Gas, or your barn, Alex?"

"I explained this to you the other night," he said, making his point with as much relentless logic as she'd used on them. "To keep all of us fighting among ourselves so we wouldn't notice the missing money until he'd had time to replace it. The fires were simply a delaying tactic."

"I'm telling you, he didn't do it." But their certainty roused another worry. "What happens if the police find Gentry and he points his finger at my father? It would be his word against Dad's."

He and Darius exchanged a brief, telling look before Alex responded. "The word of an embezzler against the word of his employee." He put it in terms that had her wincing. "Assuming Gentry doesn't have indisputable proof, it could go either way with a jury. But if I were Gentry's lawyer, I'd pound home the fact that Huntington is a thief, and a desperate one, at that. That in his position as employer, he brought considerable pressure to bear on Gentry to set the fires and promised to protect him with the Huntington name and reputation. Since the fires only caused property damage without harm to life, I suspect Gentry could get a reduced sentence in exchange for his testimony against your father."

Rebecca wondered if she looked as shell-shocked as she felt. On some level she'd thought she'd walk in here and discover it had all been a hideous mistake. That a simple conversation would clear the air. At the very least, she anticipated getting some idea of who might have done this. The fact that the evidence pointed straight at Gentry would have been cause for celebration, if they weren't so determined to link her father to his foreman.

"How do I prove Dad didn't do this?" she asked. Again, the two men exchanged glances and her anger sparked. "Look at it from my position. Assume he's innocent. There must be a way of proving that."

"We won't know anything until Gentry is found," Darius replied with stark simplicity.

She shook her head, her desperation growing with each moment that passed. "It might be too late by then. He may have figured he could use Dad as his scapegoat if he ever got caught. We need to have our own defense lined up in advance."

"In that case, I recommend you and your father hire the best lawyer you can afford."

Afford. The word impacted like a slap. She could tell Darius had said all he intended. And though he radiated patience and empathy, there was nothing more he could do for her. In fact, he'd probably said more than he should have, considering he was one of those building a case against her father. She forced herself to concede the inevitable. There wasn't any advantage to dragging this uncomfortable meeting out any further.

"Thank you, Darius," she replied. "I appreciate your frankness."

"No problem."

She would have left then, but Alex stopped her with a touch of his hand and addressed Darius. "I've been meaning to get in touch with you and Summer," he said. "I'd like to throw a small party for the two of you. I thought I'd invite the Brody brothers and their wives, Justin Dupree and my sister, and Kevin and Cara Novak. Since you eloped, none of us have had the chance to celebrate your marriage."

Darius regarded Alex with surprise and a touch of puzzlement. "That's very generous of you."

"But unexpected?"

Darius shrugged. "A bit, given your guest list."

Alex inclined his head in understanding. "I think we've all decided it's time to put the past behind us and move forward. Celebrating your marriage to Summer provides the perfect opportunity."

A huge grin spread across Darius's attractive features. "Thanks, man. I know Summer would really enjoy it. Just tell us when and where, and we'll be there."

"It'll be at El Diablo, and I'll call you with the exact date. But I'm thinking a couple weeks before Christmas? That'll make it more festive."

They all shook hands and then she and Alex returned to the parking lot. Without a word, he took her key from her hand and diverted her path toward the passenger side of the car. She didn't argue. All the fight had drained out of her. They didn't speak for the entire time it took to return to his ranch. To her surprise, he didn't turn down his drive, but continued on toward the back forty. He parked on a small hill that overlooked the bulk of his property, including the ranch house and newly con-

structed barn. Without a word, the two exited the vehicle
and wandered toward the rigorously tended fence line
edging the pasture.

"I don't know how to fix this," she confessed in a low
voice.

"It's not your problem to fix."

"I can't sit by and do nothing. He's my father."

"He's a strong, ruthless man who got himself into this
predicament. He can damn well get himself out again."

She shot him a look. "Is that what you did when your
mother was in trouble?" she asked drily. "When Alicia
had problems?"

"There's no comparison. My job was and is to protect
my family."

"Exactly. Just as it's—"

He cut her off without compunction. "You have it
backward, *dulzura*. It's your father's duty to protect
you, not the other way around."

"He has. He's protected me my entire life. It's my
turn now."

"You still don't get it." Anger underscored Alex's
voice. "He put himself in this mess. He caused it."

"The embezzlement, yes," she argued.

"And yet, even with that you're trying to take the
burden from him."

She turned on him. "What else am I supposed to do?"

"Walk away. Do nothing."

She dared to touch him. "Alex, please," she whispered. "Help us. Help me."

He stilled beneath her hand and she literally held her breath. Then he exploded into motion. Snatching her into his arms, he pulled her into an unbreakable embrace. "Just once I want you to touch me without an ulterior motive." His voice escaped, low and harsh. "Just once I want you to come into my arms without your father standing between us."

How could he even think such a thing? "My father isn't here now."

"That's where you're wrong. He's with us every minute." Alex's mouth twisted. "But you never understood that, did you? So be it. See if you understand this instead."

He bent his head and took her mouth, consuming her. Memories of the past collided with the actions of the present and merged into a confusing blend of what once had been and what now existed between them. There was sweetness from their long-ago affair. The bitterness of its ending. The lingering passion that ripped through them whenever they came together. And something else. Something more. Something new and tentative.

It was as though the fall wash of colors had grown more vibrant, filled with the promise and joy of the season. Sensation grew more acute. She became attuned to the quickened sounds of his breath and the sharp, crisp fragrance that clung to him, a combination of leather and sawdust and some incredible masculine scent she'd always associated with him. Her lips parted beneath his and she sank inward with the softest of sighs.

She'd exchanged kisses with other men. Passionate kisses. But no one had ever stirred her the way Alex did. Nor did any other man have the ability to arouse her to such heights with just a single brush of his mouth. And his hands… With typical assurance he unbuttoned her blouse. An errant breeze caught at the edges, flipping them backward and exposing the lacy bit of nothing covering her breasts.

He dragged his mouth from hers and his breath escaped in a gusty sigh. "Ivory."

She stared at him in bewilderment. "Ivory?"

His fingers drifted across her silk-covered breasts. "The color. It's been driving me crazy wondering." Before she could respond, he lowered his head and feathered a string of kisses along the edge of her bra. Her head fell back and he groaned. "I've never seen skin like yours. Like velvet cream."

His mouth drifted upward along the line of her neck until he once again delved between her parted lips. As his mouth took hers, his hands swept blouse and bra straps from her shoulders. Before the chilly air had time to bite, he cupped her breasts, the combination of cold and warmth causing them to peak against his palms. She moaned, the helpless sound a half plea. He responded by dragging his calloused fingers across the aching tips until all she wanted was to slip to the ground and complete what he'd started.

He must have felt the same because he surged against her, everything about him growing more demanding. His determined touch. The aching tenderness of his kiss. The growing need that communicated itself in every taut line of his body. No matter how much he tried to deny the fact, he wanted her. Just as she wanted him.

But almost as soon as the thought slipped into her head, he was adjusting her clothing. "There's not enough privacy," he said in response to her questioning look. "Some other time and place."

She wanted to protest his assumption, but didn't dare. If he'd taken their embrace one step further, she'd have followed. Willingly. Joyfully. Instead, she asked the first question to pop into her head, anything that would give her time to recover from what had just happened.

"What about my father?" she inquired. "Will you help me?"

It was the wrong question at the worst possible moment. All expression vanished from his face. "No." The word escaped, blunt and uncompromising and unadulterated.

She could tell he wouldn't be swayed. Couldn't be. Still, she had to try. "Alex—"

He cut her off without remorse. "Enough, Rebecca. Let me make this clear. The money is due tomorrow. If your father can't pay, he's going to jail. And I will be all too happy to put him there."

By going in person to Huntington Manor to attempt to collect the money due the TCC, he was rubbing salt in the wound, Alex decided—both his and Rebecca's. Not that his tiny epiphany stopped him.

As he turned toward the manor, a sleek black McLaren shot around the corner toward him and disappeared almost as fast as it had appeared. But even those few seconds was more than enough time for him to identify the driver.

Paulo Rodriquez.

An ice-cold fear raced through him. Rebecca had warned that she'd find someone to help them out of their predicament. Had she settled on Rodriquez, despite Alex's warning? And why wouldn't she? Since he'd turned her down, she'd have moved on to other, more fertile possibilities. And the minute she asked those other possibilities for help and received the inevitable doors slammed in her face, she'd have realized her choices were limited. Rodriquez might have seemed like the perfect solution, despite his warning.

His knock on the door was once again answered by the housekeeper, Louise. This time he was shown directly to the library where he caught the fragments of a heated argument between Rebecca and her father.

Sebastian broke off the instant Louise knocked. "What is it?" he asked, ripe impatience implicit in the question.

The housekeeper opened the door a crack. "Mr. Montoya wishes to speak with you, sir."

Sebastian swore. "Of course he does. Come on in, Montoya. Why shouldn't you put the cap on the end of a perfect day."

Alex gave Louise a sympathetic smile before entering the room. He waited for the door to close behind him before speaking. "That bad?" he asked his nemesis. He didn't wait for a response. There wasn't any point. "Allow me to put you out of your misery and make this short and not so sweet. Do you have the money to reimburse the Texas Cattleman's Club or not?"

"That depends," Rebecca responded before her father had the chance.

To Alex's private amusement, both he and Sebastian swore in unison. "How many times do we need to have this discussion, *dulzura?*" he asked. "This conversation is between me and your father."

It came as no surprise to either of them that she didn't listen. Despite the fact that she looked unbearably exhausted and stressed, she regarded them both with a strength and determination that won his reluctant admiration. Now that he considered the matter, everything about her roused a grudging admiration.

She wore a dress in the exact same shade of ivory as the undergarments from the day before and he couldn't help but wonder if it were more than mere coincidence. Her dress was elegant and deceptively simple, almost bridal in its feminine chastity, yet wickedly flirtatious in the manner in which it caressed her curves. It made his hands itch. Worse, it roused a fierce protectiveness when he realized Rodriquez had seen her looking like this.

"Will you loan us the money, Alex, and use Sweet Nothings for collateral?" she asked.

He was so preoccupied with her appearance that it took a moment for her question to sink in.

"I forbid it," Sebastian said at the same time that Alex offered a terse "No."

She lifted an eyebrow and waited a beat before filling the thundering silence that followed their outburst. "I didn't discover that El Gato came to call until after he left. I'm sorry I missed meeting him. But maybe I should get in touch with him and see if he won't loan me the money we need," she retorted calmly.

This time the two men reacted and spoke as one. "No!"

She simply lifted an eyebrow and folded her arms across her chest, waiting them out.

Alex swore again, this time in Spanish. When he'd managed to regain most of his composure, he glanced at Sebastian before returning his attention to Rebecca. "Would you mind fixing some coffee so we can discuss the situation?" he asked with formal politeness.

"I'll ask Louise to bring a tray."

"You will wait for the tray," Alex instructed. "I wish to have a private moment with your father."

He could tell she wanted to argue. Clearly, her exhaustion worked to his advantage. The fight drained out of her, leaving her pale and drawn, her only color the intense glitter of her dark green eyes and the fiery sweep of hair surrounding her ghost-white face. She gave an abrupt nod and without another word, exited the room.

Alex didn't waste any time. He turned on Sebastian. "I saw Rodriquez leaving as I drove up. What did he want?"

"That's none of your business," the older man retorted, reverting to type.

There wasn't time for this. Alex cut through the other man's bluster without hesitation. "Either make it my business or I'll leave you to deal with this mess on your own." His tone underscored his determination. He'd had all he intended to take from the Huntingtons. "You either give me the information I'm requesting or I walk out of here and leave the pair of you to learn just how ruthless Paulo can be." He shot Sebastian a hard look. "Well?"

The antagonism escaped Sebastian like air from a leaky balloon. "He wants it all," he whispered. "The manor, as well as Sweet Nothings. In exchange he'll pay off what I owe the TCC and wipe our debt clean."

"I'm not surprised."

"Because you're in on it, aren't you?" Huntington accused, working himself up into a new rage. "Because you put him up to it."

Alex stared in disbelief. "Have you lost your mind? Why would I do that?"

Huntington replied without a moment's hesitation. "You want revenge for my having fired your mother."

"An interesting theory. And though I won't deny that I'm capable of it, that isn't what happened. Rodriquez doesn't have any interest in turning Huntington Manor over to me." He paused a beat. "Any more than he's interested in owning Sweet Nothings. You do realize what he's really after, don't you?"

Sebastian turned gray. "That won't happen."

Alex merely cocked a skeptical eyebrow. "Won't it?

How much are you in to him for, Huntington? I'm guessing it's a hell of a lot more than three hundred grand."

"Closer to a million," Sebastian confessed.

"A million." Alex fought to tamp down his fury at the man's stupidity. "Where are you going to get that sort of money? How are you going to stop him from taking this house?" He drove his point home with the cruelest question of all. "What if he goes after Rebecca?"

"He wouldn't."

Alex stared at him in disbelief. "You can't possibly be that ignorant. Paulo Rodriquez is ruthless. He will stop at nothing to get what he wants. And what he wants is Huntington Manor, and now Sweet Nothings. What's next on his list? Or should I say…who? What if he adds to his demands? As far as I can see, the only question that remains is whether you're going to give him what he wants."

"Never," Sebastian said fiercely. "Not him. And not you. The manor is mine and it stays mine. It's off-limits to both of you. As is my daughter."

Alex looked at him skeptically. "I assume that means you have the money to pay off your debts?"

The answer was written in every crevice of the older man's face. "I'll find it," he bluffed, his spine as ramrod stiff as ever. "I'll take out a mortgage. People in this town owe me. They'll help tide me over."

Alex released a short laugh. There was no point in wasting his breath. Sebastian Huntington lived in a fool's paradise and only time and those people who "owed him" would be in a position to change that. "Good luck with that. It's clear you don't need my help. Let me know when you have the money. We'll expect you at the TCC first thing in the morning."

He started for the door, only to have Huntington stop him at the last second. "Wait." And then Alex caught a word he never thought he'd hear from Sebastian Huntington's lips. "Please, Alejandro. Please, wait."

It was the name his mother used whenever she'd addressed him. Hearing it come from Huntington filled him with a deep grief, chased by an even deeper anger. If not for this man, his mother might still be alive. "Last chance, Sebastian."

"Can you keep Rodriquez away from Rebecca?"

Alex turned. "I can try."

"Will you take Sweet Nothings from her?"

"I have no interest in your daughter's boutique."

"And…and the manor?"

"You would have to turn it over to me. In exchange, I'll pay off Rodriquez."

Huntington struggled with his pride before asking his final question. "Would you…would you consider allowing me to remain here? You said you have no interest in living here yourself. But this is the only home Rebecca has ever known."

"She'll get over it."

Desperation took hold. "I…I could rent it from you."

"You can't afford to rent it from me." Alex shook his head, adamant. "I want you gone, Huntington."

Huntington's hands collapsed into fists. "At least give me time."

"Time for what?"

"Allow me to remain here. Give me a year to raise the necessary funds to pay you back." Alex's expression must have been answer enough, because he waved that aside. "Fine. Six months. In the meantime, accept Rebecca's offer. Let her believe that she convinced you to loan us the money using Sweet Nothings as collateral. If I can't raise what I owe you for paying off the debt to the TCC and Rodriquez—plus interest—in those six months, the sale becomes final. You hand the deed to Sweet Nothings back to Rebecca, I'll sign the final papers giving you ownership of Huntington Manor, and I'll leave Maverick County for good. But if I manage to raise the money, you return both the manor and Sweet Nothings to us and then stay out of our lives."

Alex's eyes narrowed in suspicion. "Why involve Rebecca and her shop?"

"I don't want her to know about our deal." Huntington's mouth twisted. "She won't believe me if I tell her you simply handed over the money out of the goodness of your heart."

Alex couldn't help smiling at that. "True. She knows me too well to buy that particular fairy tale."

"Which means I need to come up with something plausible that she will believe. Her pride demands that we give you some sort of collateral in exchange for the money. And she won't give up this crazy crusade of hers if it's Huntington Manor. She'll continue to try and find another option rather than see me thrown out of my home. I can't risk her going to Rodriquez. But if she thinks you're willing to take Sweet Nothings, and that it's enough to pay off both debts, she'll back off."

Understanding dawned. "She doesn't know how much you owe Rodriquez, does she?"

"No. She believes that any money from selling Sweet Nothings—or obtaining a loan for its value—will be sufficient to pay off both debts. And I don't intend to explain otherwise."

Alex considered his options. "You realize that if Gentry implicates you in the arson fires, I won't lift a finger to help you? In fact, I'll make that a condition of the loan. If you have anything to do with those fires, the manor is mine. And nothing Rebecca says or does will change my mind."

"Since I'm not guilty I have no problem with your making that a condition of the loan," Huntington responded with impressive dignity. "Right now my main concern is paying off my debts. Are we in agreement on that score, if nothing else?"

Before they could complete the negotiations, Rebecca returned with a tray. The two men remained stoic beneath her searching gaze. While she poured coffee for the three of them, Alex gave Huntington the slightest of nods, signaling his agreement to the deal. Once the beverages had been poured and served, Rebecca stood with her saucer held in a white-knuckle grip.

"Well?" she asked.

The single word was uttered with a casual air, but Alex caught the strain welling beneath it. Carrying his coffee to the couch where they'd shared their passionate embrace just a few nights previously, he took a seat. "I've agreed to listen to your offer," he said.

"And consider it," Huntington added pointedly.

"Don't push your luck," he retorted. He didn't want to make this appear too easy or Rebecca would never buy it. "I said listen, and that's what I meant."

"It's a simple business proposition," Rebecca jumped in before her father had an opportunity to reply. "And one I hope will be to your advantage in the long run. I put up Sweet Nothings as collateral in exchange for a loan that will pay off the Texas Cattleman's Club—" She darted a swift, apprehensive glance in her father's direction. "And I'm hoping the value is also sufficient to cover my father's debt to Paulo Rodriquez, as well."

"You're asking a lot."

"I realize that." She hesitated. "Dad, would you mind if I talk privately to Alex now?"

Alex almost laughed at Huntington's expression. He had to commend the man, though. He held himself in check. Refraining from allowing the spill of words to escape, he restricted himself to a warning look before exiting the room.

The minute her father disappeared, she turned on him. "Okay, Alex. What's going on? Something's up. I can see it in both your faces. What aren't you two telling me?" she demanded.

Five

Alex offered a bland smile. "I have no idea what you're talking about."

Rebecca set aside her coffee and joined him on the couch. "You're sitting here, aren't you? Why? Yesterday you were determined to see my father go to jail. What's changed?"

Okay, he could give her that much information without her figuring out the rest. "Rodriquez."

She pinned him with a searching look. "He's that dangerous?"

Paulo might be his friend, but that didn't make Alex blind to his faults. "Yes," he replied simply. "He's that dangerous."

"This sudden willingness on your part, the fact that today you're considering my offer, it isn't about my father, is it?" she guessed with characteristic shrewdness.

"No," he conceded. "Despite my constant warnings, you keep threatening to turn to Rodriquez without realizing what sort of risk you're taking. If you go to him, you play right into his hands. Your father can't protect you from Paulo. I can."

"Why?" she whispered.

"Why am I willing to help you?"

"That and…" Her brows drew together. "Why is Rodriquez after us? What have we done to him?"

Alex chose his words with care. "Paulo's gone to a lot of trouble to dip his fingers into your father's pocket. Thanks to Sebastian's arrogance, he can't pay off both debts with what little cash he has on hand. Paulo would know that. In fact, he's probably counting on that fact. He's also not going to be happy if someone else steps in and pays off those debts after he's set everything up so he can take Huntington Manor from your father."

"You still haven't answered my question."

Fine. He'd give it to her straight. "Paulo wants status. Huntington Manor will give him that, or so he undoubtedly believes. He also wants Sweet Nothings in order to tie your hands and prevent you from using your business the way you intend to—as collateral to get your father out of debt."

"He asked Dad for Sweet Nothings, too?" Rebecca asked, appalled.

"He probably would have been willing to settle for the manor if you hadn't put yourself in the middle. I'm sure he's heard about your efforts on your father's behalf and this is his way of circumventing them."

"I couldn't sit by and do nothing."

"Actually, you could have." He waved her silent before she argued the point and placed his cup and saucer on the coffee table in front of them. "All of this is pointless to discuss. The bottom line is that both Paulo and the TCC need to be paid off or there will be consequences for both you and your father. If it were just your father, I wouldn't lift a finger to help. But for you…"

She bowed her head. "I thought you hated me."

"I'm willing to agree to your proposal. That's all that should matter to you."

She looked up at him and he could tell from her expression that she'd darted off on another path of concern. "Will Rodriquez come after you if you help us?"

"Paulo and I go way back."

She caught her bottom lip between her teeth. "Once again, you haven't answered my question. Will he come after you?"

"Are you going to put yourself between the two of us now?"

She offered a short laugh. "Apparently."

"Don't. In fact, I think I'll have my lawyer put a clause in our agreement that you'll stay away from Rodriquez or I have the right to call the note due."

Her eyes widened. "Is that even legal?"

He shrugged. "That's why I hire a team of very expensive lawyers. It's their job to make my wishes legal."

This time her laugh came more easily. Some of the strain eased from her face. "Then we have an agreement? You'll loan us the money to pay off both my father's debts, and use Sweet Nothings as collateral?"

"Yes. There might be the odd 'and, if, or but' to figure out. But we can sort that out at a later date."

She nodded. "Okay." She drew in a slow breath. "Thank you, Alex. I know this isn't what you'd either planned or wanted."

"No, it isn't."

"But I'll find a way to make it up to you. I promise."

"You can start by staying well away from Rodriquez."

She offered a small, calm smile, one that had always succeeded in driving him crazy. Unable to resist, he leaned in and cupped the back of her neck, drawing her closer. His mouth played over hers and he felt her instant surrender. With the softest of moans, she opened to him, gave as thoroughly as she received.

They drifted back against the couch cushions and he accepted this moment out of time as sheer indulgence on his part. It couldn't continue, not now that they'd agreed on the loan. But today, for this brief interlude, he'd accept what she so generously offered. As though afraid that he'd call a halt to the embrace, her fingers threaded through his hair, anchoring him in place. Unable to resist, his hands slid downward over bridal ivory, cupping the generous weight of her breast in his hand. She moaned again, just a sweet breath of sound that he drank in as though it was the most precious of nectars.

He couldn't get enough of her, wanted to discover all the ways in which she'd changed since he'd last made love to her. He swept downward over the narrow dip of her waist, the flare of her hip, to the flirtatious hem of her dress that had somehow managed to creep up toward her thighs. Slipping beneath, he found the silken length of her spectacular legs and inched upward in tantaliz- ing circles until he reached the scrap of lace protecting the heated core of her. She gasped when he penetrated the barrier and pulled her mouth free from his.

He froze at the desperate longing gleaming in her eyes, and the full weight of his actions crashed down on him. Did she want him because she had feelings for him, or because he'd agreed to loan her father the money he needed? Carefully, he eased back, feeling a distinctive chill replace the blazing heat of only seconds before.

"Why are you doing this?" he asked suspiciously.

She stiffened, disbelief stealing away her cloak of passion. "You can't seriously believe that I'm offering you some sort of down payment on your loan?" she demanded.

"You think our affair was the result of a bet. Why wouldn't you also believe I'd expect more from you than just your business as collateral? After all, I'm keeping your father from going to jail. So why wouldn't I make you part of this devil's bargain?"

She studied his face for a long, thoughtful moment, then shook her head. "I would hope you have too much integrity to do such a thing."

"Unlike before? Tell me what's changed, Rebecca."

"You've changed. I've changed. People change, Alex."

"And then, of course, there's the fact that I have money." He pulled free of her arms and stood, regarding her coldly. "Others will suspect you're paying me off with your body. You realize that, don't you?"

She sat up and adjusted the clothing he'd left in such delightful disarray. "I've never concerned myself with what others think."

He released a humorless laugh. "You will. When word of our arrangement gets out—and no matter how careful we are to keep it quiet, it will get out—we'll see how long you continue to feel that way." He walked to the door and paused. "My lawyers will be in touch. But I'm warning you, Rebecca. If you go anywhere near Rodriquez, the deal is off." And with that final warning, he left.

How had she done it? How had Rebecca managed to take his thirst for revenge and quench it with a single kiss? Alex climbed into his Jag, put it in gear and flew down the Huntington drive. The stately oaks lining the drive passed in a blur of deep autumnal russet.

He'd clearly lost his mind. Here was his perfect opportunity for revenge and he was allowing the woman who'd helped destroy his life—and the lives of his family—convince him to give it up. Again. Of course,

Sebastian Huntington had played a big part in that, since it was through him that Rodriquez had managed to get so close to Rebecca, which had forced Alex to act.

None of that changed the bottom line, he reassured himself. He had his plan in place. Granted, it was a new plan, but the end results would remain the same. When Huntington finally realized that his friends had deserted him and he wouldn't be able to finagle his way out of his current predicament, he'd be left with one choice. To sign over the deed to Huntington Manor and leave town. In the meantime, Alex would make sure the embezzled funds were returned to the TCC with interest. Then he'd clear off any outstanding Huntington debts, including Paulo Rodriquez's. He frowned at the reminder.

Paulo.

He'd have to talk to his onetime friend and find out what the hell was going on. He couldn't remember the last time they'd touched base. Maybe once in the past year, when he'd asked his old friend to keep an eye on Alicia after the arson fire. Even then, it had been by phone. But the fact that Paulo had chosen to go after Sebastian Huntington raised red flags. It was time for a face-to-face reunion.

To his surprise, he found Paulo waiting at El Diablo. He was leaning against the black McLaren he'd been driving earlier, a sleek machine that must have set him back a cool mil. He grinned when he saw Alex pull in and lifted his hand in greeting.

Alex climbed out of his own vehicle. He crossed to Paulo's side and gave him a hard hug. "Good to see you, man."

"My address hasn't changed any more than I have." He lifted an eyebrow. "Maybe it's you who's changed, eh? Maybe the barrio isn't good enough for you anymore?"

"You know that's not true."

They'd just chosen different paths in life. Paulo's wasn't one Alex cared to follow. He's always assumed they'd both understood that fact and made peace with it. Now he wasn't so certain.

Paulo let the comment pass and inclined his head toward the barn, still in the process of being rebuilt. "Problems?"

"Nothing I can't handle." And it wasn't. Once Huntington's complicity in the arson fires had been proven beyond a shadow of a doubt—and despite the man's protests, Alex suspected it would be—there would be retribution. And it would taste sweet, indeed. He deliberately changed the subject by gesturing toward the McLaren. "I see you've bought yourself a new toy."

It was the perfect distraction. "It's just in. I think I own the only one like it in the entire state." Paulo's avid gaze ran over the sleek lines of the car, examining it with more passion than he would a woman. "Make my day, Alejandro, and tell me you aren't just a little envious."

"Maybe a little." Alex smiled. "Though I'd think you'd choose something a bit more subtle, something the cops don't instantly peg as belonging to you."

Paulo clasped his hand to his chest. "You wound me, *amigo*. The cops have no reason to stop me. I'm a legitimate businessman these days."

"I gather that includes your business with Sebastian Huntington?"

An expression of amused delight appeared on Paulo's face and his grin flashed white. "I wondered when you'd figure that out. Accept it as a gift from an old friend."

Alex stiffened. "Tell me what you've done."

"Consider it payback for what Huntington did to you, little Alicia and *Tía* Carmen."

"You scammed him."

Paulo gave an impatient click of his tongue. "He was easier to train than a dog. I said, 'roll over' and he asked how many times. Even after the first deal went bad, he came back begging for more. He made it easy. Too easy."

Damn it. Damn it. Damn it! Alex forced a smile to his lips. "Come inside and have a drink while we discuss it."

"Nothing to discuss." Paulo rubbed his hands together. "Soon, you and I will both own big Texas homesteads. You will sit in your El Diablo, while I am lord of Huntington Manor." His eyes took on a frenetic glitter. "And when I submit my application to the TCC, you will get me approved. You and my beautiful new wife."

Alex didn't like how this was going down. Not even a little. "Congratulations. I didn't know you were engaged."

"Oh, I'm not. Yet. But I have a feeling Rebecca Huntington will do almost anything for her dear *papá*. Especially if it keeps him out of jail, yes?"

"Becca?" he said, stalling. It confirmed his worst suspicions.

"I've wanted a taste of her for a long time." Paulo's eyes narrowed. "You wouldn't deny me that taste, would you, *mi amigo?* Not considering I was honorable enough to keep my hands off her while you took your fill a few years back."

"Honorable."

The word tasted like acid in his mouth while fury burned in the pit of his stomach. The mere idea of Rodriquez putting his hands on Rebecca had the most base and brutal instincts ripping through him. The bitter irony tore him to shreds.

His friend was right. Chances were, Rebecca would do anything to save her father. Hadn't she all but offered herself to him in exchange for his help? And hadn't he taken advantage of that fact not even an hour ago? How did that make him any better than the man standing before him? At least Paulo was honest in his desires, while Alex had wrapped his up in the pursuit of revenge and justice.

"There's only one problem, Paulo," Alex found himself saying. He could only pray he could pull this off without incurring his old friend's wrath. "I've agreed to pay Huntington's debts. If you'll tell me what he owes you—"

"Have you lost your mind? This is the man who made your life a misery. The man who destroyed your family. The father of the woman who—" He stopped dead and swore. "Of course. The woman."

"It's done. Let it go and walk away."

"*No!*" Paulo cut him off with a slicing sweep of his hand. "That's not going to happen. I've worked too long and hard to allow that *cabrón* to escape vengeance."

"He didn't do anything to you. It's not your revenge to take."

"Don't you understand?" Paulo's retort bit sharp in the quiet night air. "I'm doing this for you. I'm doing this for your sister. For your mother."

Alex refused to allow the lie to stand. "You're doing this because it's the only way you can force Rebecca into your bed."

Paulo's expression turned ugly. "Do not interfere, *hombre.* We have been friends a long time. But no one, not even one I consider *mi hermano,* takes what I regard as mine."

"Rebecca Huntington isn't yours. She never was and she never will be." Alex stepped closer, ignoring the way Paulo's hand shifted to the back of his jeans. There was only one way to get through to a man like Rodriquez. "The lady belongs to me. Her father belongs to me. Huntington Manor belongs to me. And I will protect what is mine."

Rage swept across Paulo's face, ripping apart any remaining shreds of civility. "You are making a mistake, Montoya." He tore open the door of his McLaren and slid in, gunning the powerful engine. "A big mistake."

Hitting the accelerator, he forced Alex to jump to one side as he sent the car screaming down the drive, a

rooster tail of gravel kicking up in his wake. Getting the
nicks and scratches out would cost him a pretty penny,
which wouldn't help his mood any. Alex glanced across
the yard, surprised to see his foreman, Bright, standing
on the portico of the sprawling ranch house, a shotgun
leveled in the direction of the retreating taillights.

"He had a gun," Bright called. "Tucked in the back
of his belt."

Paulo always had a gun tucked in the back of his belt,
but Alex didn't bother to explain that fact. He lifted a
hand. "Thanks, Bright. Everything's fine."

For now. But for how much longer? Not only did
Alex have to deal with Paulo Rodriguez, but he'd now
committed himself to paying off the TCC debt—along
with whatever Huntington owed Rodriquez. Even more
pressing, he needed to make a decision about Rebecca,
as well. Was he going to prove he was as savage as
Rodriquez by sacrificing his honor and taking what
she'd offered? Or was he going to do what his mother
would have considered the "noble" thing and help the
woman he'd once loved?

His intellect strained toward noble. Unfortunately,
the rest of him wasn't listening.

Rebecca unlocked the front door of Sweet Nothings
and flipped the discreet sign in the window from "Please
visit later" to "Please come in!" She'd already started
the coffee percolating on the vintage serving table that
separated the retail area of the store from the section

containing the cozy sitting area and the dressing rooms. And she was literally counting the minutes until the freshly ground beans finished brewing. She'd managed two whole hours of sleep last night and it showed. Thank God for makeup, since it managed to hide most of the damage.

She couldn't decide whether to be relieved or dismayed when the morning started out dead slow. At least it gave her time to put out a shipment of new inventory and catch up on her billing. She was on her third cup of coffee when the bells above the doorway released a light, sweet chime, signaling her first customer of the day. To her delight, it was Kate.

"Thank goodness it's you." Rebecca headed for the silver service and topped off her own coffee, then poured a second helping into another delicate Lenox cup and saucer. She handed it to her friend. "All I've gotten whenever I call is your voice mail."

Kate accepted the coffee with a grateful smile. "I know, I know." She took a sip and moaned. "I swear you make the best coffee in the entire county. Maybe the entire state."

Rebecca took a restorative sip and then handled the situation the way she always did—confronting it head-on. "Okay, what's up? I can tell when you're trying to avoid something, and you have avoidance written all over you." She mentally braced herself. "What's going on? I've left a thousand messages. Why haven't you gotten back to me?"

Her friend winced. "I'm sorry. Things got crazy after lunch the other day."

"So, you have been ducking my phone calls."

Kate held up a hand. "Only until Lance got his facts straight. Plus, I wanted to be with you when we spoke."

Rebecca stared in dismay. "It's that bad?"

Sympathy swept across Kate's pretty face. "Yes," she stated bluntly. "It's that bad."

"If this is about the TCC accounts…" It took every ounce of resolve for Rebecca to meet her friend's eyes. "I know about it and it's true."

"Oh, sweetie!"

"The money will be replaced," Rebecca stated emphatically. "Every last dime. Alex has agreed to loan us the money in the meantime."

"Alex?" Kate looked as amazed as Rebecca felt.

"See what you miss when you don't return my calls?" Her flash of humor died and she met her friend's gaze. "I'm determined to see he's paid back as quickly as possible, even if I have to take on a second job to do it."

Kate caught her lip between her teeth. "There's something else you should know. I'm not really supposed to tell anyone, but you should have some warning."

"It's about the arson fires, isn't it?"

"Yes." Kate caught Rebecca's arm in hers and guided her to the divan adjacent to the tea table. "Sit before you fall down."

"He didn't do it." Tears welled up in Rebecca's eyes and she blinked fiercely to hold them at bay. She wasn't a crier, but between her father's confession, the interludes with Alex and the lack of sleep, her self-control was pared down to a mere thread. "I swear, Kate. Dad's admitted to taking the money, but he swears he had nothing to do with the refinery fire or Alex's barn. And I believe him."

"Of course you do," her friend said in a soothing voice.

"I know he's not the easiest man to like," Rebecca confessed with difficulty. "He's hard and…and arrogant. And he's made mistakes. But he wouldn't endanger lives."

"Darius Franklin is looking into it. I trust him. He's a good man. He'll get to the bottom of everything."

"I spoke with him the other day and I agree with your assessment. He is a good man. He…he advised we get a lawyer." Without warning, Rebecca dissolved. Her cup rattled against the saucer and Kate rescued it before the fragile porcelain could shatter. Without a word, the two embraced and rode out the storm. At long last, Rebecca pulled back and wiped the tears from her cheeks.

"I'm—"

"Don't you dare apologize," Kate said in a fierce voice. "After all the times you stood by me while I wept over Lance, don't you dare. You hear me?"

Rebecca managed a watery smile. "I hear." Behind them, the bells above the door sang a gay greeting and she flinched. "Will you cover for me while I fix my makeup?" she asked in an undertone.

"Of course." Kate spared a quick glance over her

shoulder. "Oh. It's Alicia Montoya. She and Justin will be tying the knot soon, won't they? She's probably here to pick out something for her wedding night."

"Let's hope that's all she's here for," Rebecca murmured.

Not waiting for a response, she hastened into the back to the small powder room. She groaned when she looked in the mirror. Black mascara tracks streaked her face and left crescent moons beneath her eyes. She looked like a zebra, her face dead-white in between the black stripes, while her eyes and nose were red and swollen. The downside to being a redhead. Everything showed on her face.

She took her time washing up and reapplying her makeup. Then she loosened the formal knot of hair and allowed the auburn strands to flow loose around her shoulders. Better. If Alicia looked closely, she wouldn't be able to miss the hint of red that lingered around Rebecca's eyes. But with luck, it wouldn't be readily apparent. Taking a deep breath, she exited the powder room and returned to the front section of the store.

Kate and Alicia had their heads together, deliberating between two nightgowns. Kate held the first, a sexy little black number that revealed far more than it concealed. Alicia clutched the second, a deep ruby gown that gave an extra luster to her lovely olive complexion.

"Is this for your wedding night?" Rebecca asked as she joined them.

"Yes, it is." Alicia gave her a shy smile. "I've wanted an excuse to buy lingerie here for a long time."

Rebecca returned Alicia's smile with surprising ease, probably because the other woman had a knack for making people feel comfortable. "Yes, I remember you telling me that when you were in here a while back with Cara. But you didn't have anyone special to wear it for." She gave a wide smile. "Until now. Congratulations."

"Thank you." She returned to deliberating between the two choices. "I just can't decide whether to go full-out sexy with this black one, or more modest with the red."

"If you're asking my advice…"

"Yes, please!"

"Go with the red. The black may look sexy, but it's too blatant for a wedding night. One look and all your secrets are revealed. You want more romance. More mystery. And watch…" She draped the material over Alicia's arm. The feather-light material clung, while the light seemed to sink into the gown, turning the silk almost transparent against her skin. "Justin will be able to see through the gown just enough to drive him crazy."

The next hour passed in a flash. Helping Alicia choose lingerie for her wedding and honeymoon proved a delightful distraction. Afterward, while Rebecca rang up the stack of purchases and Alicia looked on with a shell-shocked expression, Kate discussed wedding details.

"Have you decided whether or not you're holding the wedding at El Diablo?"

"That was our original thought, but after the incident with the barn, Alejandro has changed his mind. We've decided to marry at the mission church."

"Just because of the fire?" Kate asked in concern. "Is he worried about another incident?"

"Not since Darius installed security. But after the fire, Alejandro's housekeeper quit and he's had a terrible time finding a replacement." Alicia shrugged. "It just made more sense to switch the venue to the church. Besides, it's a beautiful old place, all stone and timber. And we've decided to have the ceremony on Christmas Eve after Eucharist."

"I can't think of anything more perfect," Rebecca said with all sincerity.

She finished ringing up Alicia's purchases, then wrapped them in tissue and placed the lingerie in a series of elegant boxes. But all the while her brain spun in circles, replaying that one sentence over and over again. *Alejandro's housekeeper quit and he's had a terrible time finding a replacement.* An idea formed. A crazy, impulsive, outrageous idea.

The minute Alicia left the shop, Rebecca turned to Kate. "I know the perfect person for Alex's housekeeper. And the best part about it is that it will kill two birds with one stone."

Kate stared in utter bewilderment. "What in the world are you talking about?"

"Not what. Who."

"Okay, I'll bite." Kate smiled indulgently. "Who would be the perfect person for Alex to hire as his housekeeper?"

"Me."

Six

Alex tucked his hammer into his tool belt. Stepping back from the barn, he settled his Stetson more firmly on his head to shade his eyes from the late-afternoon sun and stared up at the towering structure. Almost done. Soon, no one would ever know there had been a fire here.

He always found hard physical labor satisfying. It also had the added benefit of easing some of the pent-up anger and frustration from his encounters with Huntington and Rodriquez. The temptation to allow the two men to destroy one another was overwhelming. He'd actually consider it, except for one thing.

Rebecca.

Desire continued to rip through him after his latest encounter with her. He'd hoped that working on his barn would ease it. Instead, a bone-deep hunger gnawed at him, warning that this wasn't an emotion he could expunge from his system through sweat and determination. It would require far more than that. Even so, his labors had clarified one thing.

Sebastian Huntington would pay for what he'd done. And Rebecca was going to end up back in his bed—but not in order to settle her father's debt.

"You've got company," one of his hands said, inclining his head toward the gravel drive.

Sure enough, a faint plume of dust rose in the distance. A few minutes later, a sporty convertible pulled into the sweeping circle fronting the ranch house. It didn't take much guesswork to figure out who sat behind the steering wheel.

He took his time joining Rebecca. She stood with casual elegance beside the door of her Cabriolet and waited him out. She wore a sexy little dress in a stunning bronze that made the most of her figure and showcased a pair of legs that were among the prettiest he'd ever seen. The setting sun caught in her hair, turning the rich red to a halo of vibrant color around her face. She wasn't wearing sunglasses and the vividness of her green eyes hit like a shock as he approached. She stared at him, as proud and indomitable and self-assured as ever. Well, that made two of them, both too headstrong for their own good.

He shoved his Stetson to the back of his head. "I'm almost afraid to ask, but what are you doing here, Becca?"

She straightened, facing him with a determination that made him instantly wary. "I've come to solve two of our most pressing problems."

Hell. "If this is about your father—"

"It's about my father's debt, to be exact."

"By all means, let's be exact."

He might as well have saved the sarcasm. She brushed it aside the way she would a pesky mosquito. "Alicia came into my shop today and mentioned that you've been without a housekeeper ever since the fire."

He took the odd turn of conversation in stride, merely folding his arms across his chest and cocking an eyebrow. "So?"

"So, you'll be relieved to know that won't be an issue any longer."

The comment caught him by surprise. In order to give himself time, he stripped off his gloves and hooked them in his belt. Then he leveled the playing field by closing the short distance between them and tipping her face up to his. "What are you up to, *dulzura?*"

If he hadn't been near enough to see the hint of alarm flashing through her gaze or to hear the slight hitch in her breathing, he'd have thought her unaffected by his touch. "Meet your new housekeeper," she informed him. "I'll accept whatever wages you were paying your former live-in and I'll stay until my father's debt is paid off."

He couldn't help himself. His mouth twitched into a broad smile. "You're joking."

She pulled free of his grasp and reached inside the car to push the trunk release. "I'm also giving you my car. That should put a small dent in what's owed. I bought an old pickup as a replacement since I'll still need to get to the boutique." She circled to the rear of the car and wrestled the first suitcase free, dumping it on the gravel drive. "I'm afraid I'll have to spend part of each day at Sweet Nothings, but my assistant is well-trained and I can arrange my hours to suit your convenience. I'll also get up early to take care of the main housekeeping duties and then finish them off after work and whenever the store is closed."

"Enough, Rebecca," he insisted with a hint of impatience. "I don't know what game you're playing, but I'm not amused."

She whipped around with a ferocity that shocked him. "This isn't a game. Nor is it funny. In fact, I find nothing about the events of the last twenty-four hours the least bit amusing."

"I'm not hiring you."

She must have anticipated that small hurdle, because she had her counterargument already lined up. "You won't be able to resist, Alex. Just think how delicious it'll be, telling everyone that Rebecca Huntington is your new housekeeper. Where once your mother was housekeeper to the Huntingtons, now the last of the Huntingtons is housekeeper to you." Turning her back on him, she hauled out the rest of her possessions, stacking them neatly on the ground. "Now, if you'll show me to my quarters and give me a rough idea of my duties, I'll get some dinner on the table for you."

She bent to gather up the first load and he snatched the suitcases from her hands. Son of a bitch! They weighed a ton. What the hell had she filled them with, rocks? "You're not staying, and you damn well aren't going to play at being my new housekeeper."

She stepped in front of him to prevent him from returning her suitcases to her trunk. "I intend to pay off my father's debt one way or another. I'm going to hand over every spare penny from the shop and work the rest of it off here, Montoya, one day at a time, until the debt is paid in full."

"That's Mr. Montoya," he shot back. "My employees address me as *Mister* or *Señor,* or even Alex. But they all address me with the proper respect or they find a job elsewhere."

She inclined her head with a dignity and grace that was an innate part of her. The fact that it also filled him with a bizarre combination of pride and desire left him at a loss for words. "You're right. I apologize, Mr. Montoya."

He swore in Spanish. "This is ridiculous." She'd realize just how ridiculous if she knew the full extent of the debt. "I can't have you working for me, Becca. You must see how it'll look. What people will say?"

"Let them talk," she retorted fiercely. "They're going to, no matter what I do. As you've already pointed out, my reputation is in tatters. And I don't see how my presence can possibly hurt yours."

Didn't she get it? He spelled it out for her. "People will say you're my mistress, not my housekeeper."

Her eyes blazed like emeralds. "But I'll know the truth. My friends will know the truth. You'll know the truth. As far as I'm concerned, that's all that matters."

He hesitated.

When Rodriquez had left the previous night, he'd been furious. He'd also been determined to make Rebecca his. At Huntington Manor, she was vulnerable. Here, where he could keep an eye on her, she'd be safe, or reasonably so. Granted, she'd still have to go into town each day and work at her shop. But he didn't think even Paulo would have the nerve to do anything to her in broad daylight within the confines of a busy store. And wasn't her safety paramount?

As a rationalization, it barely passed muster. But he couldn't quite get past the image of Paulo's face when he'd spoken about Rebecca. There'd been no mistaking the man's intentions, just as there was no mistaking one simple fact.

Alex would do anything to keep Rebecca out of Paulo's hands.

He gave it two full seconds of careful consideration. "Fine. You're hired."

She didn't bother to conceal her triumph, though that would be short-lived. The minute he explained the full extent of her duties, he expected her to pack up her overstuffed suitcases, chuck them into the trunk of her car and scurry off down the road as fast as her fancy little sports job would take her.

When she reached the steps leading to the front door, she paused and he caught the first hint of vulnerability. She turned toward him. "Maybe we should start the way we intend to go on," she said.

"What are you talking about?" He shot her an impatient look. "Could we move this along? These suitcases aren't getting any lighter."

"I'm your housekeeper, Alex." She gave a quick shake of her head. "I mean, Mr. Montoya."

"Alex," he said sharply.

"Housekeepers don't usually enter through the front door," she pointed out. "Your mother never did. Not after the day you first arrived."

"Oh, for the love of—" He tromped up the steps, juggled the suitcases and managed to drop one on his toe. He practically kicked open the door. "In," he ordered.

Beside him, Rebecca opened her mouth again, no doubt to argue some more. "But—"

"Madre de Dios! You don't have the first clue how to be an obedient, respectful employee, do you? Is it your intention to argue over every single request I make?"

She stared at him, stricken. Then a hint of laughter crept into her eyes and her lips quivered into a full-blown smile. "Not if they're requests."

He dropped her suitcases in the foyer and succeeded in avoiding his toes this time. He slammed the door shut, sealing them in the dusky interior. Without a word, he swept Rebecca into his arms, intent on proving to her in the simplest, most straightforward manner available the sheer insanity of her idea.

"You know what they'll call you, don't you?" he warned.

She didn't struggle. Nor did she sink against him. "I believe you said I'd be labeled the daughter of a thief."

"Now they'll call you Diablo's mistress."

She met the ferocity of his gaze with surprising equanimity. "We'll know the truth."

"And what truth is that?"

She stood within the warmth of his embrace, their heated breaths mingling, their hearts beating as one, and said, "That I'm just your housekeeper, nothing more."

He took her words as a challenge. And then he took her mouth, intent on proving her wrong. This was a mistake, Alex conceded an instant later. Rebecca had only been in his home for thirty seconds and already he had his hands on her. Hell, all over her. He was practically eating her alive. Not that she resisted. She should have slapped him. Instead, she slipped her fingers into his wind-ruffled hair, knocking his Stetson to the parquet floor, and secured him in place so that their mouths melded, one to the other.

He couldn't get over the flavor of her, the delicious appeal that was so distinctly hers. His hands swept downward, sliding over territory he'd spent bitter, lonely years dreaming about. The shape of her had changed since those long-ago days. Subtle changes that had transformed the girl he'd once known into the woman he now held.

Her breasts still filled his palms, but her body had grown leaner, more honed and better defined. Her hips flared beneath the narrowest of waists and her backside had just the perfect amount of curve to it. He wanted to slip his hand beneath her skirt and discover whether she wore another sampling of the sweet nothings that gave her lingerie shop its distinctive name. Sultry black bits of nothing or maybe siren-red. Perhaps she'd chosen the same sort of dainty ivory scraps of sweetness he'd seen before. Silk and lace that melted against her creamy skin and set off the blazing nest of curls between her thighs.

The image his brain created threatened to unman him. He didn't want to take her here in his foyer, though if they didn't find a suitable arena for their activities, that was precisely what would happen. More than anything, he wanted to carry her to his room and spread her across his bed while he stripped her down to those delicate morsels of feminine finery and find out just what color she'd chosen to wear today.

Intent on turning thought into deed, he eased back in order to sweep her into his arms. Instead, he gave her just enough breathing room to come to her senses. With an exclamation of disbelief, she ripped free of his embrace.

It took her a moment to regain her breath enough to speak. "This has got to stop," she informed him. "I'll be

your housekeeper and do the best job I know how. And
I'll even deal with any gossip that occurs as a result. But
I'm damned if I'll become your mistress in anything
more than imagination."

"Too late, *dulzura*. We're both damned already." He
leaned in. "And you will become my mistress. It's only
a matter of when."

God help him, but she was beautiful, especially when
angry. She glared at him with those witch-green eyes.
The deep, lustrous red of her hair spilled around her
face, emphasizing the creaminess of her skin and under-
scoring the flush that rode the sweeping arch of her
aristocratic cheekbones.

"If you'll show me to my room?" she asked in her
best lady-of-the-manor voice. "I'd like to unpack before
I start dinner."

"Yes, ma'am," he said in his driest tone. "This way."

He headed for the back of the sizable ranch house.
Near the kitchen, he opened the door to the suite of
rooms that had belonged to his former housekeeper. He
carried her suitcases through to the bedroom and set
them on the floor near the bed. He glanced up in time
to see an odd look on her face.

"What?" he asked warily.

"This can't possibly be the housekeeper's quarters," she said.

"That's exactly what they are."

Her expression turned unreadable as she walked
through the pair of bedrooms, each with its own bath,

and then into the generous-size living area. When she finished, she looked at him with eyes gone dark with pain. "These rooms weren't at El Diablo before you moved in, were they?"

"No."

"You had them built specifically with a housekeeper and…and whatever family she might have in mind." She didn't wait for his confirmation. "This is because of Huntington Manor."

He flashed back on the single room that her father had grudgingly split in two so that he, his mother and sister wouldn't all have to share a single bedroom. There'd also been a living area, but it had been so tiny there'd barely been space for one, let alone two teenagers and their exhausted mother.

It hadn't taken long to figure out that the only reason Huntington had accommodated them with even that much was to avoid any whisper of gossip. Image was everything with Sebastian Huntington. Image. Reputation. Appearances. It wouldn't do to have someone accuse him of mistreating the hired help, particularly since Alex's mother had cleaned most of the homes in Somerset at one point or another and was well-liked by all. But that didn't change the fact that the spaciousness of Huntington Manor stopped short at the servants' quarters.

Another flush swept across her face, this one deeper than before and having nothing whatsoever to do with passion. "I'm sorry, Alex," she said. "I'm sorry for what my father did to you and to your sister because of our affair. But I'm most sorry for what he did to Carmen. It was wrong."

He folded his arms across his chest. "I'm surprised you're not defending him, or at the very least offering a string of excuses. Isn't that part of your role as his daughter?"

She sighed, revealing a hint of weariness. "Not in this case."

Now that he looked closer, he could see the exhaustion in the paleness of her skin. Dark smudges underscored her eyes, intensifying the color. It gave her a vulnerability that made him long to take her in his arms again. But he didn't dare. Not here. Not when her father's actions still stood between them.

"Take the night to get situated. You can start work in the morning."

Her shoulders straightened and her spine snapped into an unrelenting line. "That's not necessary. Just tell me what you want."

He took a single step in her direction. "You already know what I want."

Alarm flared for a brief instant before a hint of humor replaced it. "I'll be happy to check in the refrigerator, but I can say with some degree of confidence that that particular item isn't on tonight's menu."

"Put it on the menu," he advised. "Soon."

He exited the room before he put it there for her. He forced himself to keep walking, to stride out of his home and return to the barn. Once there, he'd put in another solid hour or so of hard physical labor. Maybe then he'd be too exhausted to think about what awaited him back at El Diablo and what he'd like to do to and with her when he returned. His mouth compressed. Who was he kidding?

He'd never be that exhausted.

The evening rapidly went from hideous to total nightmare in the space of two short hours.

Rebecca stood in the monstrous kitchen of El Diablo and faced facts. The few cooking skills Carmen had taught her during her teen years had totally deserted her. Lack of practice, no doubt. She'd aimed to serve Alex a simple but filling dinner of Texas-size steak, charbroiled on the outside and still mooing when sliced. A large salad. Baked potato. And homegrown beans with almond slivers. The only part of what ended up hitting the table that remotely resembled her game plan was the salad.

The steak hadn't been charbroiled, but crispy-crittered. The potato was stone-cold in the middle, and hard as a rock. And the beans were great alps of green mush with almond chunks clinging to the mountaintop like jaw-breaking boulders. Alex had taken one look, closed his eyes and muttered a prayer beneath his breath before digging in. Five minutes later, she noticed that he'd added a generous serving of whiskey to the menu to help wash the mess down.

Rebecca surveyed the endless stack of dishes still to be scoured and fought an overwhelming urge to weep.

Enough of that! She'd chosen to do this and she'd succeed no matter how difficult. She refused to quit. She refused to back down. And she absolutely, positively refused to fall into any bed but her own.

Searching through the various drawers and cupboards, she located an apron and rubber gloves and set to work. She'd check with Alex once she finished and get a list of the chores his previous housekeeper had covered. In order to get them all done and still arrive at her shop by nine in time to open the doors, she'd have to get up early. Very early.

She was just loading the final dish into the dishwasher when Alex appeared in the doorway. "Thanks for the meal," he offered.

She sighed. "That's generous of you, all things considered." She turned to face him and tugged off gloves. "Do you have a minute to give me a list of my duties?"

"Won't take even a minute. Clean the house. Keep up with the laundry. Fix breakfast and dinner. Don't worry about lunch. I usually eat out."

"I assume you also need me to do the grocery shopping?" When he hesitated, she planted her hands on her hips. "Did my predecessor do it?"

"Yes."

"Okay, then."

"Becca—"

"Please, Alex," she whispered. "I have to try. Give me a chance."

The mouth she'd taken such delight in kissing compressed into a hard line. "You know as well as I do that you can't do an adequate job around here and still run Sweet Nothings. It's too much for one person."

"I can manage until I get the debt paid off."

He shook his head in disbelief. "Do you have any idea how long that's going to take?" he demanded. "We're not talking about a few weeks or months. We're talking about years."

"Not necessarily. The shop provides an excellent income. You should be able to get a decent amount for my car. It may be used, but it's been gently used."

"You're living in a fool's paradise, Rebecca. You won't be able to keep up this pace for a month, let alone years. Face facts."

Rebecca struggled to regain her footing. Maybe she'd have a better shot at it if she weren't so tired she could barely see straight. "You think I haven't? You think I don't know how much we owe you?" Struggling for control, she pulled out a chair at the kitchen table and sat as carefully as though the least careless movement would shatter her. She moistened her lips before continuing. "I'm not quite the fool you take me for, Alex."

He studied her warily. "What do you mean?"

"I realize that if you hadn't agreed to use Sweet Nothings as collateral that you'd now own Huntington Manor." She waved a quick hand through the air. "You, or someone other than my father. Someone like Rodriquez. Dad would have been forced to sell in order to cover his debts and lawyer fees."

"Probably."

"It could still happen," she whispered. "Couldn't it?"

He started to reply, then broke off with a shrug. "Don't worry about it."

"Alex?" she pressed.

"Let's just say this mess is far from over." His expression was more grim than she'd ever seen it. "Until it is, stay away from Rodriquez, Becca," he ordered. "If he contacts you, refer him to me, and then call me immediately."

"Is my father in danger?"

"Madre de Dios!" Alex forked his fingers through his hair. "Paulo is dangerous to *you,* Becca. That's all that should concern you. Your father made his bed. Let him learn to sleep in it."

"Is that the attitude you'd take if our situation was reversed and Carmen was the one at risk?" she dared to ask.

He made a valiant effort to control his temper, which impressed the hell out of Rebecca. "As I've pointed out before, that's not a fair comparison and you know it. First, my mother would never have put herself in the position your father is in. There were times when she couldn't put sufficient food on the table, but she never resorted to stealing so much as a penny from any of the fine mansions she cleaned, even though they could well afford it and would never have missed the odd bits and pieces that would have made the difference between filling our bellies and going hungry."

"Oh, Alex," she whispered, her heart breaking for him.

His head reared back. "I'm not asking for your pity," he said in a cutting voice. "I merely state fact."

"Let's say that your mother had borrowed money from Rodriquez to tide you over, and was then unable to repay it. You'd have stepped in before he could harm her." There wasn't a doubt in her mind. "How is what I'm doing any different?"

He crossed the room in a half dozen swift strides and plucked her from her chair. "The difference is that your father is well able to look after himself, even if he now chooses to hide behind your skirts. The difference is that my mother was a kind, loving, humble woman, while your father is an arrogant bastard who thinks he can do whatever he pleases without taking responsibility for his actions or suffering the consequences for them."

She wished with all her heart that she could deny any one of his points, but she couldn't. As much as she loved her father, she wasn't blind to his faults. That didn't mean she wouldn't stick by him and do her best to help him out of his current predicament. The full enormity of the task pressed down on her like a crippling weight. Paying back the TCC—or rather, Alex—had seemed tough enough. But now that he'd explained about Paulo Rodriquez...

"Enough," Alex announced. "It's clear that you're at the end of your rope, and I won't have people saying that I'm responsible for driving you into the ground."

She started to wave that aside, letting out a gasp of surprise when he swung her into his arms and carried her out of the kitchen and into her private quarters. He didn't pause, continuing straight through to the bedroom. There, he dumped her onto the mattress and cupped the back of one ankle, and then the other, in order to slip her shoes from her feet.

"I can undress myself," she informed him with a dry smile. It was either that or weep. "I've been doing it for more than two decades."

"And here I thought you had servants to take care of that, as well as grant your every other whim."

"Funny." She pointed toward the door. "I believe I've made it clear where my duties end. And it's on the other side of that door."

He continued to hold her ankle for a long moment. His fingers drifted over the narrow bones, teasing the sensitive skin until she shuddered with the effort to control her reaction. To her profound relief, he didn't seem aware of how close she came to tugging him down on top of her and allowing desire to overrule common sense.

"A pity." Alex released her ankle and stepped back. He paused halfway to the door and glanced over his shoulder. "You will remember to call me if Rodriquez contacts you in any way?"

It wasn't worth arguing about, not when every instinct she possessed urged her to do just that. "I promise."

"Sleep well." His mouth tugged to one side. "God knows, I won't."

Seven

The next week proved one of the most stressful Rebecca had ever experienced. Exhaustion dogged her every step. It wasn't just getting up at four each morning in order to take care of her housekeeping duties before racing into town to open Sweet Nothings. She hadn't taken into consideration the sheer manual labor involved in keeping a mansion the size of El Diablo in pristine condition.

Well, if she looked at the bright side of things, she could cancel her gym membership. Her daily workouts there were nothing compared to what she received cleaning and dusting the endless rooms that comprised Alex's home. She just had to give herself time to adjust. And she needed time to learn the most efficient way to clean.

Until this week, she'd never considered her shop a place to rest and relax. But now she treasured every precious hour she spent there, especially knowing what awaited her back at El Diablo. It wasn't that she minded the physical aspects of the work, despite how exhausting they were. It was the quiet forbearance with which Alex regarded her efforts.

He ate her under-over-badly cooked food with a stoic air. He didn't complain when she bleached the color out of his shirts or tinted unexpected color into them. He didn't do more than sigh when his boots stuck to the polish she'd spent hours applying to his wooden floor. But with each incident, she felt less and less capable and more and more as though she were taking advantage of him. He shouldn't be paying her. She should be paying him for all the damage she'd inflicted on him and his home.

Rebecca forced herself to her feet with a heartfelt sigh and proceeded to unload the latest shipment of lace and silk delicacies. Though the beginning of the week had been as busy as ever, the past few days business had slacked off. She suspected the recent cold snap was in part to blame. Who wanted to purchase silk lingerie when the weather screamed for fleece?

Behind her, the bell tinkled merrily and a customer wandered in, someone Rebecca vaguely recognized from high school. "It's Mary Beth, isn't it?" She greeted the woman with a friendly smile and gestured toward the section of the store she'd just finished organizing.

"The items on the rack beside you are just in. In fact, you're the first to see them."

"Probably the last, too," she said in a cool voice.

Rebecca stared in confusion. Maybe if she hadn't been so tired, she'd have caught on sooner. Instead, she offered a puzzled look. "Excuse me?"

"Business a bit slow?" Mary Beth ran careless fingers over the latest shipment, knocking several of the garments off their padded hangers. "It's only going to get slower now that all of Somerset knows the truth about you mighty Huntingtons. Who's going to want to buy sleazy underwear from someone like you?"

Rebecca froze. "I don't know what—"

Mary Beth cut her off with a wave of her hand. "Oh, please. It's all over town. Your father. You working for Montoya." She made annoying little air quotes around the word "working." "And won't we all just have the biggest laugh while we watch you tumble off your pedestal." She gave the store a dismissive look. "Enjoy your Sweet Nothings. Without customers, that's precisely what this place will be. Nothing."

She swung toward the exit, just as the door opened. A man standing there ran an appreciative glance over Mary Beth. *"Señora,"* he murmured, flashing a brilliant, white grin at her.

She returned the look with interest, then stepped into the November chill. Rebecca could only pray that she didn't appear as shell-shocked as she felt. Gathering her self-control, she offered the new customer her most professional smile. Now that she looked at him, he seemed vaguely familiar, as well. Dread swamped her. With luck, he'd prove to be a legitimate customer and not some curiosity seeker reacting to the rumors that had apparently begun circulating about her and her father.

"May I help you?" she asked warily.

His mouth curved upward in an oddly satisfied smile. "In more ways than you can count," he murmured in a lightly accented voice. Aware that his comment had thrown her, he gestured toward the interior of the store. "I'm looking for something special. For my future wife," he clarified.

"I can help you with that."

"I'm sure you can."

His comment caused a visceral reaction she couldn't explain, but one that sent warning alarms clamoring. She did her best to conceal her concern and moved toward the front of the store, rather than the back. "Could you give me some idea what you're looking for?"

He gave it a moment's consideration. "A nightgown. For our wedding night."

"And your fiancée's coloring?"

A slow smile lit his face, one that didn't quite reach his hard, black eyes. "Why, she's a redhead, like you."

Okay, she knew when someone was playing games with her. And this guy was definitely a player. And then it hit her where she'd seen him before. It had been a brief glimpse several months ago. He'd been talking to her father, the two in a rather heated discussion. When she'd asked her father about the incident, he'd brushed it aside. Now the incident took on greater significance. If she were a betting woman, she'd lay odds this was the infamous Paulo Rodriquez, which could only mean one thing.

Trouble.

As casually as she could, she picked up her cell phone from the counter by the register and bounced it from hand to hand in what she hoped appeared to be a restless, unconscious habit.

"Hmm. Well, black always looks—" She blinked, as though in surprise. "Hang on. My phone is vibrating. Damn. It's Alex. If I don't take this…" She broke off with an irritated shrug.

Before he could react, she flipped it open and hit the 1 key assigned to automatically dial Kate's cell. At the next opportunity, she was going to program Alex's private number into her phone. To her profound relief, her friend picked up almost immediately. "Yeah, Bec. What's up?"

"Yes, Alex. I'm fine." She rolled her eyes in an exaggerated manner. "You worry too much."

There was a beat of silence. Then, "Something's wrong, isn't it?" Rebecca could only thank God that she'd picked smart friends. Kate wasn't slow in putting two and two together and coming up with "Help!"

"You said Alex. Is he there? Is he causing the trouble?" she asked.

She could only hope the note of irritability she forced into her voice would cover up her fear. "No, no. I'll be home at the usual time."

"No, of course not. That wouldn't make sense. You wouldn't have used his name if he were there with you," Kate muttered. "That can only mean you want me to call him."

"Yup, that's it. Listen, I'm with a customer and I don't want to keep him any longer. So stop calling me."

"I'm out at Brody Oil and Gas. I'll call Alex. And then Lance and I are on our way."

"Whatever. Goodbye, Alex." For some reason, just saying his name out loud helped steady her. Unfortunately, it had the exact opposite effect on the man flicking through the rack of nightgowns. She took a deep breath and asked brightly, "I'm so sorry. Where were we?"

"Ah, yes. This." He held up a sheer baby-doll nightie in blazing red. "This will look beautiful against your skin."

"Your fiancée's skin," she corrected with a smile. "And if she has hair similar to mine, that particular shade of red will clash."

He returned the bit of silk and lace to the spiral rack. "A shame. I am quite fond of this particular shade. Perhaps something in green." He plucked an emerald-green costume at random and slowly approached. "To match my soon-to-be fiancée's eyes."

Rebecca froze. She edged backward, but the man moved with lightning speed, putting himself between her and the exit. He flicked the lock on the door and then casually picked up the welcome sign and reversed it. Then he smiled in a way that sent a wave of terror pouring through her veins.

"Paulo Rodriquez, I assume," she managed to say.

"It is a pleasure to finally meet you, Señorita Huntington." His cold smile flashed. "But considering how close we're about to become, why don't I call you Becca?"

"Because only my friends call me that. And you're not one of my friends."

"I could be." He glided toward her, trapping her against the counter. "I *will* be."

"What do you want?"

"Your father owes me a great deal of money. I think it's time I was paid a small down payment." He closed in. "Let's call it…an interest charge."

Alex hit the sidewalk outside his office building at a dead run. It was faster to walk—or run—to Sweet Nothings than to drive there, Alex decided. Plus, he didn't want to alert Paulo to his presence until he walked through the door. He didn't know how Lance Brody had become embroiled in whatever was going on at the lingerie shop, but he owed the other man for calling with the warning. It was a debt that wouldn't easily be repaid.

The small placard in Sweet Nothing's window read, "Please visit later" and drove a shaft of fear straight through the core of him. From what he could see of the interior through the tinted glass, the inside stood dark and silent. Gathering his self-control, Alex tried the door. It was locked, but he made short work of that. Even after all these years, some of his less-reputable skills came back with amazing swiftness. Opening the door, carefully so the bell wouldn't give his presence away, he walked in. For an instant, he didn't see or hear anything. Then a muffled cry came to him from the small divan in the sitting area of the store.

He didn't recall moving. One minute he was in the front of the shop, the next he was in the rear with Rodriquez on the floor, bleeding. He glared at Alex through a rapidly swelling eye and ran his tongue across his split lip.

"You shouldn't have come," Paulo said.

He'd switched to Spanish, no doubt to keep Rebecca from understanding what he said. Alex decided to accommodate him. "I warned you not to touch what belongs to me. You should have listened."

Paulo shifted and Alex stepped closer, shaking his head. With a groan, the other man settled back on to the floor. "And you should have listened to me, Montoya. I will do whatever I must to have the woman. To have her home. To have the status that once was hers." He smiled, despite the pain it must have caused him. "To have her in my bed, heavy with my child."

The image burned like fire in Alex's mind, no doubt as intended. He forced himself to ignore it, not to allow it to distract him. Just as he forced himself to ignore Rebecca. If he looked at her, he'd lose it. Big-time. "She's in my home now. In my bed. And that's where she's staying. If you want payment for Huntington's debts, I'm the man to see."

"You would really pay off his debts, after all he's done to your family?"

"Yes." Alex smiled coldly. "Like I said, Paulo. You can't win. Now get out before the lady presses charges."

"She won't do that." He tossed Rebecca a knowing look. "There's been enough gossip. If anyone hears about this… Why, they might just wonder whether the lovely Becca is helping her father pay off all his debts. And in a tradition as old as time. Eh, Alejandro?"

"Basta!" Alex ended the conversation by hauling Paulo to his feet and swiftly disarming him. "Where are your men?"

"I'm alone."

Alex dismissed that with all the contempt it deserved. "You haven't been without bodyguards since you were twelve. I repeat. Where are your men?"

"Out back." He fingered his lip and winced. "Next time I will post them at the front door, as well."

"There isn't going to be a next time, Paulo. Now get out and take your men with you before I call the cops."

Paulo shot a lingering glance in Rebecca's direction before exiting the shop. The instant Alex deemed it safe, he crouched down in front of her and gathered her ice-cold hands in his, rubbing her fingers to warm them. "Are you okay?"

It took her a nerve-racking moment to respond. "Shaken, rattled and rolled. But I'll survive."

Her stab at humor would have been more reassuring if her face wasn't bleached white and her eyes weren't so frantic. They'd turned a green so dark they reminded him of an impenetrable jungle wall, closed off from light and easy ingress. In fact, now that he looked carefully, he realized she had closed down.

He continued to rub her hands and talk to her in a low, calm voice. All the while, he examined her. The attack had been brief, if terrifying. The first two buttons of her blouse were ripped, exposing the plum lace of her bra. Her skirt was hiked up to her thighs, but he knew that had occurred when she'd kicked Paulo while Alex was dragging him off the divan. He noticed a few bruises marring her pale skin, one on her neck and one on her knee. The rest of the damage was psychological, rather than physical.

He had no idea how long he crouched there. Behind them, the bells above the door tinkled in alarm and she jumped, panic stricken. Lance and Kate slammed into the shop.

"Is she okay?" Kate demanded. "Bec?"

She flew to her friend's side and wrapped her up in a tight embrace. Alex slowly rose, feeling impotent and angry. He spared Lance a quick look, surprised to catch an expression of sympathetic understanding in his dark eyes.

"She was attacked?" Brody asked in a low voice.

Alex nodded. "Rodriquez," he answered quietly. Leaving her in Kate's capable hands, he shifted toward the front of the store where Rebecca couldn't overhear their conversation.

"Were you in time?" Lance asked.

"Yes. Though he left plenty of damage in his wake."

"This doesn't sound like a problem that's going away anytime soon." Brody frowned. "How are you going to handle it?"

"I haven't quite decided," he admitted. "But I won't have Rebecca put at risk."

Lance planted his fists on his hips and studied the floor. "Are the rumors true?" he asked bluntly. "About you and Becca? Is she living with you now?"

"She's my housekeeper, nothing more."

Lance swore beneath his breath. "That's low, Montoya. Even for you."

"Do you think I had any choice?" he shot back. "She showed up on my doorstep, bags in hand."

"You could have—and should have—sent her packing."

"As it turns out, El Diablo might be the safest place for her."

"Not likely. She's fast becoming a laughingstock. Her reputation is in shreds. And the fine, upstanding 'ladies' of our fair town are talking about boycotting Sweet Nothings."

It was Alex's turn to swear. "She's just trying to pay off her father's debt."

"It's how she's paying it off that has people talking."

Alex glared at Lance. "You've wanted a piece of me for a long time now, Brody. Keep poking and you'll get your wish."

He waved aside the offer. "Calm down. I'm not saying anything that isn't flying all over town. Becca doesn't deserve this. And I'm telling—*asking* that you fix it before any serious damage is done."

"I'll handle it, Brody." But right now he had something else to handle. He crossed to where Kate and Rebecca were huddled. "I'm taking you home, *dulzura.* We can either close the shop or call your assistant. Which would you prefer?"

"That bastard isn't going to win. I refuse to shut my store down," she stated in no uncertain terms. Her ferocity relieved him as nothing else could have. "I'll call Emma and ask her to cover for me."

"Why don't you come and stay with me and Lance?" Kate offered. "Just for a day or two."

It took every ounce of willpower for Alex to keep his mouth shut when he wanted to simply step in, sweep Rebecca into his arms and carry her back to El Diablo. It wasn't his choice to make. If staying with her friends would make her feel better, then he'd pack a bag for her himself and send her on her way.

"Thanks, anyway," Rebecca said. "I'll be fine at Alex's."

"She'll be more than fine," Alex stated. "I'll see to it, personally."

"Besides," she continued. "I'm behind on my housekeeping. This will give me a chance to catch up."

Two sets of accusing eyes ripped into him. Alex simply shook his head. "That's not going to happen. You need time to recover from your shock."

"No," she corrected firmly. "I need something to

keep my mind occupied so I'm not sitting around dwelling on it."

"We'll argue about it later." He urged her to her feet. "My car is back at Montoya Imports. Do you think you can walk that far?"

"I wish you'd all stop treating me like an invalid. Of course I can walk that far," she snapped.

By the time they arrived at the ranch, she'd recovered both her color and, along with it, more of her fight. "I really do need to get some housework done, Alex."

"As your employer, I forbid it."

"Forbid." She blinked as she absorbed the word. "Did you really just use the word 'forbid' with me?"

He shot her a quick grin. "Only as your employer."

"Seriously, Alex. What do you expect me to do?"

He pulled into the sweeping circle and parked by the steps leading to the front door. If he could have driven right up onto the porch, he would have. "I expect you to relax. You've worked very hard this past week. You've earned a day off."

Alex exited the car and circled around to open the passenger door. Rebecca climbed out. To his concern, she appeared pale again. Shadows smudged the delicate skin beneath her eyes like faint violet bruises. In the unrelenting glare of the late fall sunshine, he could see the exhaustion that shrouded her. His mouth compressed. He should have stepped in long before this. She couldn't keep playing at being his housekeeper and manage Sweet Nothings. It was too much for any one person.

"Come inside." If the words sounded more like an order than a request, he didn't give a damn. Whether Rebecca liked it or not, she needed rest and he'd see to it that she got it. "I don't know about you, but I could use some coffee."

Her eyes brightened at the suggestion. "That sounds perfect. I'll make some."

"You brew excellent coffee, but I plan to add something you don't."

"What's that?"

"Wait and see."

Together, they headed for the kitchen. He pointed to one of the chairs and waited for her to reluctantly take a seat. Once she'd complied, he slipped off his suit jacket, rolled up his shirt sleeves, and started the coffee. While it brewed, he poured a hefty dose of whiskey into a pan and gently warmed it until it was piping hot. Then he carried mugs, brown sugar, the heated whiskey, and the coffee to the table where she sat.

"Okay, I'm intrigued."

"Forget intrigued. Prepare to be impressed."

He poured coffee into each of the mugs, added the sugar and stirred the mixture. Inverting the spoon so it faced downward, he slowly poured the hot whiskey over the curved back. When he finished, he crossed to the refrigerator and pulled out whipped cream, topping each drink with a healthy dollop.

"Irish coffee," he informed her, nudging one of the mugs in her direction. *"Sláinte."*

"What does that mean?"

"It's Gaelic for 'to your health.'"

Her eyes glittered with laughter, chasing the shadows away. "Okay, I'm officially impressed."

"You'll be even more impressed when you taste it. Give it a second to cool and then see what you think."

He'd sparked her curiosity. "That good?"

"Better."

With a laugh, she buried her nose in the mug and took a cautious sip. "Oh," she murmured. She lifted her head and gazed at him, wide-eyed. "Oh, my."

He chuckled at the sight. Reaching out, he swiped a smear of whipped cream from the tip of her nose. How was it possible that she could look so beautiful? The lingering traces of fear and panic had left her pale and drawn. The whipped cream added a bizarre element of silliness to the contours of her face. And yet, she still took his breath away. She appeared almost ethereal in her aspect, especially with the blaze of red hair that tumbled to her shoulders and the impossibly green eyes glittering in delight. If she hadn't been so strong-willed and passionate, he'd have thought her a delightful pixie who'd decided to drop in for a dram of the whiskey he'd slipped into the coffee.

"How in the world did you learn to make this?" she asked.

"My previous housekeeper was Irish. She taught me."

Rebecca grimaced. "You must miss her, especially considering that her replacement doesn't come close to matching her high standards."

"I'll survive," he said with lazy assurance. He sipped his own coffee. "But you're right. I do miss her. Mrs. O'Hurlihy was a gem."

Rebecca released her breath in a gusty sigh and put a serious dent in her coffee before responding. "I know there's a lot of room for improvement, but I am trying."

"I'm aware of that. And to be honest, I can't think of anyone better suited to organize the party I'm planning to celebrate Darius and Summer's marriage. As I recall, you used to put together some rather spectacular events for your father."

For some reason, she withdrew ever so slightly. The smile she offered appeared strained and tight. "I'd be happy to take care of it," she said. "Though I would like to suggest you hire caterers, if you don't object. I'm not sure my cooking is quite up to par for what you have in mind."

"I would have hired caterers even if Mrs. O'Hurlihy were still with me. I just need you to decorate and oversee everything."

"Of course." Her nose disappeared into the mug again. "Who…who do you plan to invite?"

"The usual crowd. The Brodys, Alicia and Justin Dupree. Mitch and Lexi. Kevin and Cara Novak. Maybe a few others, too."

"Will this be a formal dinner?"

"No. Let's keep it casual. I'll arrange for you to have some strong backs to help with the Christmas decorations and the tree. I'm thinking we should serve dinner buffet style." Collecting her empty mug, he crossed to the stove and put together another round of drinks, making sure he gave Rebecca a generous helping of whiskey in the hopes it would further relax her. He set the drink in front of her, pleased when she immediately picked it up and took a sip. "This place actually has a big fancy ballroom. I think I've set foot in it once. But see if it won't work for the party."

"I'll get on it first thing in the morning."

Something in her voice sounded off and he studied her in concern. "Okay, what is it? What's wrong?"

She tossed off the question with a shrug. "Nothing. Just tired."

Guilt flooded through him. He was a selfish bastard. Here he was dropping a huge party on her after she'd just been attacked. What the hell was he thinking? He took her mug from her hands, surprised to find she'd already emptied the contents.

"Bed," he stated emphatically.

Not giving her time to argue, he swung her into his arms and carried her through to her living quarters. She rested against his chest and for the first time he realized just how fine-boned and downright fragile she felt against him. Easing her onto the mattress, he started to pull back when her arms tightened around his neck. Then she lifted her face to his and feathered a kiss across his mouth.

"Stay," she whispered. "Please, Alex. I don't want to be alone."

Eight

Rebecca clung to Alex, tightening her hold when he started to pull away again.

"Please, Alex," she said again. "Don't go."

"You don't know what you're asking." His voice sounded rough.

"I know precisely what I'm asking."

"It's the whiskey talking. And the reaction to what happened with Rodriquez."

She shook her head and held on, soothing the tension rippling across his back and neck with a gentle kneading motion. "Don't bring him into this. Not here. Not now. This is just for the two of us to share."

"There is no 'us.'"

"Who are you trying to convince, me or yourself?" She laughed softly and caught his bottom lip between her teeth. Ever so gently she tugged. "There's always been an us, from the first time you walked into Huntington Manor." Old, sweet memories flooded through her. "You came swaggering in, this tough, angry teen from the barrio, and I knew my life would never be the same."

He sank against her, the smallest of surrenders. "You were just a kid."

"I'm only two years younger than you. I was…" She searched for the appropriate word. "Teetering."

"Teetering?" His smile flashed white in the duskiness of the room. "Sweetheart, you were all woman, even then. Slender, graceful, that incredible hair of yours a silken waterfall of deep rose. You stood along the second-floor railing, looking down at us in the foyer. A princess inspecting the peasants."

"Never," she instantly denied. "I never felt that way and I never will. I remember looking at you and thinking… Why, there he is. He's the one."

"And I remember looking at you and wondering if your skin really was that white or if it was just a trick of the lighting. And thinking how much I wanted—" His smile faded. "That's when your father told us that the help didn't use the front door. We were to go around to the back."

"Oh, Alex," she whispered, feeling his pain. "I know there's nothing I can say to make up for his attitude."

"Don't even try."

"I don't intend to. In fact, I don't intend to say much of anything. Instead, I'd rather act."

She lifted upward and captured his mouth with her own. Slowly, she drew him closer until he fell heavily into her embrace, his weight a delicious pressure. For a long time, she indulged herself in a thorough exploration of his mouth. His kisses had always been intoxicating, but now they were even more potent than the whiskey he'd poured into their coffee.

He'd changed in a number of ways since they'd last been together, she realized. His shoulders were broader and the muscles across his back and along his arms harder and more sharply defined. He'd also filled out, his torso wider and more solid than the whipcord leanness she remembered with such clarity. Even his face was different. Distinctive brackets were etched into either side of his mouth and laugh lines crinkled at the corners of his eyes. Though his features had never possessed a particularly youthful aspect—at least not in all the time she'd known him—when last they'd been together, he hadn't quite attained the mantle of command that now cloaked him.

Intent on familiarizing herself with this new Alex, she took her time, allowing her fingers to wander over his face, to skim across the furrows and climb into the shallow indent dividing his chin. All the while he studied her, his expression watchful, his eyes the exact shade of bittersweet chocolate. Memories flitted there, some that allowed tenderness to slip through, others that held him at a distance. She accepted it. Understood it. After all, didn't she feel the same?

Rebecca lifted upward again, her mouth following the path her fingers had taken. She had a choice. She could give him a final kiss and send him on his way. And he'd go. She didn't doubt that for a moment. Or she could listen to the dictates of her heart and finish what she'd started. It took no thought at all.

She didn't know when—or if—this opportunity would ever present itself again. Chances were excellent that morning-after regret would prevent a reoccurrence. But just for today, she couldn't bear to turn him away. Their romantic interlude wouldn't lead anywhere. She knew that. Too much stood between them. But they could have right now. They could have this brief time together. And when it was over, she'd deal with the fallout. She'd even walk away, if he insisted, because she'd still have the memories to take with her.

The instant she reached her decision, she stroked her hands downward, finding the buttons of his dress shirt and releasing them one by one. His skin felt warm against her own, and the firm, steady beat of his heart seemed to gather within her palms of its own accord. Slowly, she pushed the crisp cotton from his shoulders and down his arms. He stopped her before she could remove it altogether.

"Are you sure?" he asked. "No regrets afterward?"

She offered him a teasing smile. "Of course there'll

be regrets, on both our parts. But I'll deal with them. And so will you."

"You've had too much to drink. It's been a traumatic day for you. I should—"

"You should tell me whether you still keep an emergency condom in your wallet."

She saw the answer in his eyes and smiled in a way that had him swearing beneath his breath. He shoved his hand into his back pocket and pulled free his wallet. She took it from there, removing the foil packet before tossing his billfold to the floor, followed by his shirt. Then she reacquainted herself with every inch of him, memorizing anew all the corded ridges and smooth, rippled expanse of him. When she grazed his belt buckle, he toed off his shoes, allowing them to drop to the floor with a decisive thud, signaling his unconditional surrender.

"You strike me as a woman who's a bit overdressed for the occasion," he informed her.

"Maybe you should do something about that."

"My thoughts exactly."

He channeled his energy into remedying the situation. With the ease of experience, he had the zipper of her skirt undone and the lightweight wool following the path of his shirt and shoes. She lay beneath him clad in the silk and lace products of her trade, a delicious advertisement for him and him alone.

"I wouldn't have thought you could wear that shade of plum. Not with your hair. But it works." He shot her a slow grin. "It really works."

"So I noticed."

She made short work of unfastening his belt and un-zipping his trousers. He eased back and she reluctantly let him go while he removed the last of his clothing. Then he returned to the bed and ran a finger along the low-cut edge of her bra.

"Still overdressed," he observed.

"Still waiting for you to do something about it," she retorted. "Or shall I?"

She didn't wait for him to decide, but wriggled out from under him and stood. Taking a swift step back-ward, she evaded the arm he shot out to snag her. She crossed to a nearby chair and lifted one foot onto the seat. Deliberately taking her time, she released her stocking from her garter and rolled it down her leg. A low groan emanated from the direction of the bed. She turned her attention to the next stocking before removing the garter altogether and draping the various pieces of sheer femininity over the back of the chair.

"Come to bed and let me finish that," Alex demanded.

"Don't get up," she insisted with mock solicitous-ness. "I'll take care of it."

One by one, she lowered the spaghetti straps of her bra, which seemed to drift of their own accord down her arm. Then she released the catch at her back and inch by excruciating inch allowed the lacy scrap to fall free. Alex released a harsh exclamation and exploded from the bed. In one swift move, he had her off her feet and falling through the air onto the mattress.

Sunlight stroked her skin, and then it was Alex stroking it. Her. She tilted her head back and closed her eyes, reveling in a touch that combined tenderness with a tormenting aggression. He cupped her breasts and then took possession of them with lips and teeth and tongue. She arched beneath him, wanting more. And he gave it to her.

His hands plied across the softness of her belly to the final triangle of silk still covering her. She felt the delicate waistband snap and the next instant, the silk had been torn away, leaving her completely open to both his gaze and possession.

Sunlight danced along the auburn nest protecting the heated core of her. Murmuring in Spanish, he slid his splayed fingers into the curls, arousing her even further with a probing touch. Ever so carefully he spread her, teased her to the very brink. She clung to her sanity just long enough to rip open the foil packet he'd given her earlier and slip the contents over him. And then he was breaching her, sliding inward with a single, deep thrust.

"Alex!"

"I'm right here, *dulzura*." His breath escaped in a hot gust. "I'm with you all the way."

She closed her arms and legs around his powerful form and clung to him, rode with him, melded with him. The sunlight around them intensified, so bright it blinded her to all but the man within her arms. He became her everything, filled her with all that he was. And she gave up to him, surrendering every bit of what she felt within her heart and body, until there was no more to give.

And in that final moment of climax, they became one, no longer separated by the past, but joined by it. Until that instant she'd truly believed that their connection had ended a long time ago. But as she tumbled toward bliss, Rebecca realized that the love she'd felt for Alex had never truly died. It had simply waited dormant for this time and this place and this man to rise again, like a phoenix from the ashes. The love she felt for him hadn't gone away.

And in that incandescent moment, she realized it never would.

She didn't know how long they slept. It was dark when she awoke, disoriented. She no longer lay in Alex's arms, though the warmth from his body lingered, indicating he'd only recently left her. From the depths of the room she caught the quiet movements as he gathered his clothing.

"Alex?" she murmured.

"Go back to sleep, Rebecca."

The formality dismayed her. He'd called her Rebecca. Not *dulzura*. Not even Becca. He'd thought she'd be the one with regrets the morning after. It would seem that he'd beaten her to it, and it wasn't even morning yet. She lifted onto one elbow.

"Are you all right?" she asked gently.

He froze, then released a sound that was part sigh and part laugh. "I believe that should be my line."

"Probably," she conceded. "But I'm not the one sneaking out."

"I wasn't sneaking," he instantly denied. "I was trying not to wake you. There's a difference."

"Mmm. Only a man could come up with that sort of distinction." She swung her legs over the side of the bed. "You're sorry this happened, aren't you?"

She caught the shadow of his head turning in her direction. "Aren't you?"

She considered for a brief moment. "I'm sorry that I've become a cliché," she admitted. "But I'm not sorry we made love."

"And only a woman could make that distinction."

"Probably." She released her breath in a sigh. "Would you prefer we pretend this didn't happen?"

She sensed his sudden stillness. "You're joking, right?"

"No, I'm not."

She wrapped the sheet around herself and switched on the bedside lamp. A soft pool of light enveloped her. Dragging the sheet from the bed, she stood and faced Alex. To her disappointment, he regarded her with a wary, remote gaze. Where was the man who'd shared her bed, who'd made love to her with such intense passion? Long gone, apparently.

"Look…" Alex ran a hand through his already rumpled hair. "It happened. We're both adults. We've been here before."

"And will again?" she dared to ask.

He shook his head a bit too promptly. "There's too much between us, Becca. It wouldn't be wise."

Well, at least he was calling her Becca now. A slight

improvement. "In case you hadn't noticed, wisdom isn't my strong suit."

"We can't go back."

He made the statement with such gentleness that tears pricked her eyes. "I'm aware of that. I was actually thinking of moving forward. You know." She lifted her shoulder in a shrug, catching the sheet before it could slip to the floor. "We're at a crossroads and all that. We can't go back, but we can go forward. It's how we move forward that's in question."

"I won't turn you into a town joke. If we start an affair, people will pick up on it. They'll see it in the way we look at each other. Or speak. Or touch." He bent and snagged his wallet off the floor where she'd dropped it and tucked it into his back pocket. "Alicia didn't have to say a word and I knew she and Justin were together just from how they interacted."

"I don't care about gossip."

"I do and you will."

He stated it with such implacability that she knew no amount of argument would sway him. "All right. We won't make love again."

"You'll see. It's the right decision," he said. "The only decision." Picking up his shoes, he crossed to the bedroom door. There, he paused and glanced at her over his shoulder. "You okay?"

She smiled reassuringly. "I'm fine."

He took her at her word and left. The instant the door closed, her smile faded. Well, what had she expected?

That he'd fall at her feet and declare his undying love? That he'd beg her to marry him and have his babies? She sank onto the edge of the mattress and closed her eyes. Damn.

His babies.

Once upon a time, it had seemed not just a possible dream, but a likely one. Now it was as much an improbability as her reaching for the moon and plucking it from the nighttime sky. Curling into a ball, she reminded herself that she wasn't going to have any regrets. If all he could give her was this one night, then she'd thank heaven above for the memory and be grateful she'd been given that much.

Unfortunately, she hadn't planned on falling in love with Alex again. Too bad she hadn't considered the likelihood of that beforehand—not that it would have made a difference. If she lived to be a hundred, the memory of this one special night would bring a smile to her face whenever she thought of it. And she planned to think about it a lot. With that final thought, sleep claimed her. When it did, it was with a smile on her lips.

And a tear on her cheek.

Everything changed over the next week. Alex turned into her employer—a real employer. And Rebecca found keeping a smile on her face more difficult than she imagined possible. When he scheduled a formal meeting with her in his office to discuss the upcoming party, Rebecca was determined to prove to him that she could handle the aftermath of their…

She hesitated to call it an actual affair. A one-night stand? Whatever the term for it, one thing was certain. Alex was determined to hold her at a careful distance.

"I want to discuss the Franklin reception with you," he said when she joined him in his office. He waved her toward the chair in front of his desk and folded his hands on the tidy teak surface while leveling her with a detached stare that buried all hint of emotion. "You've handled these sort of affairs for your father, haven't you?"

"I've organized them, yes," she agreed cautiously.

He lifted an eyebrow. "Okay, I know a 'but' when I hear one."

She hesitated. "In the past, I've always hired a caterer."

"Which I've already given you permission to do," he replied with an edge of impatience.

She sacrificed tact for honesty. "I'm not sure I can handle all my normal responsibilities in regard to maintaining the house in addition to covering everything that needs to be done for the party, especially since you want the place decorated for Christmas."

"Got it." For the first time, a hint of emotion slipped through his impassive demeanor. The fact that it was amusement she took as a good sign since it returned them to a more companionable footing. "You have my permission to hire extra staff if you need it. You can supervise staff, I assume?"

She grinned. "I excel at it."

He returned her smile with one of his own and that's when she saw it—a blistering flash of desire that came and went so quickly she thought maybe she'd imagined it. Right until she saw his fingers tense. And for the first time since their night together, she felt a resurgence of hope.

"Fine. Your new job is to take care of the party." He shoved back his chair. "If you'll excuse me, I have to get back to work."

She stood, as well. When he made to pass her, she touched his arm. Just that. He paused, staring down at her with keen regret. "We can't, Becca," he informed her gently. "It won't lead anywhere good."

"Funny. I thought our night together was pretty darn good. More than, if you want my opinion." This time he didn't reveal any amusement. Instead she caught regret, and that more than anything filled her with sorrow. Without another word, she let him go. "Right," she whispered when he was no longer within earshot. "I get it."

It wasn't until she was in the middle of discussing the meals with the caterer that she saw her conversation with Alex in a far different light. Rebecca had worked successfully with Angie, the owner of the company, in the past, but her new position as Alex's housekeeper seemed to change Angie's attitude toward her. There was a slight hint of discomfort that Rebecca was finally forced to confront.

"Okay, Angie. What's going on? You and I have worked together a dozen times in the past. What's the problem?"

Angie sighed. "I'm sorry, Rebecca. It's not your fault. It's mine."

"Is it because I'm Alex's housekeeper?" she asked bluntly. "Or is it because of my father? What's the deal?"

"I can't pretend I haven't heard the rumors, but I know you. If your father did something unethical, that's on him," Angie replied just as bluntly. "I don't hold it against you."

Rebecca blinked in surprise. "Thanks. I appreciate it. But…if that's not the problem, what is?"

"It's Montoya. Rumors are flying all over Somerset about his forcing you to be his…housekeeper," she spoke the word with a telling edge to her voice, "in exchange for helping your father. I'm just not sure I want to work for someone capable of doing such a thing."

"Is that all?" Rebecca said with a relieved laugh. "Then let me reassure you. Alex didn't force me to work for him. If anything, it was the other way around."

It was Angie's turn to blink. "Come again?"

"I showed up on Alex's doorstep and told him I'd work as his housekeeper until my family's debt is paid. He did everything he could to talk me out of it." She grimaced. "If what you're saying about the rumor mill is accurate, I'm beginning to understand why he was so reluctant to take me on. I had no idea people would think he'd forced this on me."

"I have to tell you, this certainly puts a different light on things."

"Good. I'm glad." Rebecca smiled. "Alex is really a great guy. Maverick County is fortunate to have him living here."

DAY LECLAIRE   149

"Fair enough," Angie said, though a hint of doubt remained in her voice. "But won't it be weird for you?"

Rebecca shook her head in confusion. "I don't understand. Won't what be weird?"

Color darkened Angie's cheeks. "Won't all your friends be at this party?"

"Most of them, sure. So?"

"Well, won't it be weird being one of the hired help instead of a guest? I'd think it would be really awkward. For you *and* them."

Rebecca couldn't believe the thought hadn't occurred to her before this. It would be awkward. She spent the rest of the day considering it and trying to find some way out of her predicament. Maybe she could arrange for the extra staff she'd hired to cover for her.

Then she shook her head. The party was her baby and hers alone. Dumping the job on someone else wasn't fair to Alex or his guests, particularly Darius and Summer Franklin. Besides, everyone would only be uncomfortable if she made them feel that way. If she treated it as par for the course, so would they.

She hoped.

Rebecca considered calling Kate and explaining the situation, but feared her friend would end up leading a protest that would ruin the party. She'd feel awful if a reception meant to celebrate the Franklins' marriage turned into something unpleasant. All of which meant that she needed to rely on every ounce of poise and good humor to carry off the evening.

The next few weeks flowed by while the house took on more and more of a holiday aspect. Fresh greenery, poinsettias, vases of fresh-cut winter flowers and swags in winter-green and burgundy festooned the house. With the help of a workforce of willing backs, the ballroom became a winter fairyland that delighted everyone who saw it.

The day of the party, she took extra pains to make sure everything was set up properly. Angie arrived with her catering staff and began to prepare the dishes for the buffet. Toward the end of the day, Alex passed her in the hallway on his way to his room and paused long enough to compliment her on how beautiful the house looked. He even surprised her—and himself, she suspected— by planting a fleeting kiss on her lips.

"Thank you for all your hard work. The place looks amazing."

"Thanks."

He drew back, though she could see it was a struggle to revert to the role he'd assumed over the past few weeks. "Guess I'd better get showered. Guests arrive soon."

"I think that's my cue to get changed," she said lightly.

"I'll meet you back here in forty-five."

Hastening to her room, she debated over her choice of clothing. She didn't want something that looked too much like a uniform. No point in rubbing people's faces in it. But at the same time, she didn't dare wear anything that smacked of a cocktail dress. She needed to draw a subtle line between staff and guest without causing tension. Finally, she settled on a simple black skirt and black silk blouse.

Precisely fifteen minutes before the first guests were due to arrive, she stationed herself in the foyer where she could greet Alex's guests and escort them to the ballroom. She carried a tray of champagne to offer each couple as they arrived and was in the process of finding the best place to position it when she heard Alex's footsteps on the sweeping stairway behind her. He halted halfway down. She turned to smile up at him, but to her alarm, he stared at her in outrage before finishing his descent.

Crossing to her side, he grabbed her arm, jarring the tray. "What the hell do you think you're doing?"

Nine

Rebecca struggled to hang on to her dignity, but she could feel fine cracks forming, expanding with each second that passed. "I'm getting ready to serve your guests," she replied, amazed at how calm she managed to sound.

He snatched the tray from her hands and slammed it onto a nearby table. The crystal sang in protest at his rough treatment and champagne splashed over the edges of the fragile flutes. "I don't know what game you're playing—"

"Game?" To her shock, fury shot through her, a fury she didn't even realize she felt until that moment. "I'm not the one playing games. I'm your housekeeper.

You assigned this job to me. I'm simply doing what you pay me to do."

He glared at her in open affront. "I am not paying you to offend our friends and neighbors by acting the part of a servant. Go change into an appropriate outfit and then join us for the celebration."

"Why?" she insisted. "So I won't humiliate you? I'm not ashamed of my job. Why are you?"

His eyes narrowed dangerously. "Is this your way of getting even? Is this because I haven't pursued a relationship with you after we made love? You feel the need to wear sackcloth and ashes because you've become, in fact, what people are calling you behind your back?"

She could feel the blood drain from her face. "How dare you?"

"How dare *I?* How dare *you* put me in such an embarrassing position with people who are more your friends than mine? Who have spent the last decade barely tolerating my presence in the community?"

Understanding crashed down on her and she began to realize she'd made a terrible mistake. That somehow, maybe because of what Angie had said to her, she'd misunderstood his intention. And now she'd insulted him. Truly, deeply offended him.

It had never occurred to her that he felt so uncomfortable around people who had been her friends for most of her life. And it should have. Hadn't she seen how difficult the Brodys had made his life through the years? How he'd been treated by some of the more elitist of those with whom they'd gone to school, who would have considered it beneath them to associate with the son of a housekeeper? In that moment, she saw herself through his eyes and felt incredibly small and petty even though she hadn't been deliberately trying to embarrass him.

"I'm sorry, Alex. I swear I never meant to put you in such an awkward position."

"And yet, here you stand," he snapped, "on the verge of shredding my reputation."

She stared at him in utter bewilderment. "Excuse me? How would this affect your reputation?"

A mask fell over his expression, cold and forbidding. "How do you think my guests will react when you answer the door dressed like that? If you play servant to my lord of the manor? They will take one look at you and walk out of my home." He thrust a hand through his hair. "Don't you get it? My reputation is all I've ever had. Whatever I've earned has been through that and sheer hard work. Endless days and nights of it. And I won't have you or anyone else destroy in one single night what I've spent decades building."

"That wasn't my intention," she said stiffly.

"In that case, you have a choice, Rebecca. You can retire for the evening, or you can put on a dress, along with a pleasant expression, and join your friends while they celebrate Darius and Summer's marriage. Or are you so determined to show everyone what a total bastard I am that you'll go to any length to prove it?"

A knock sounded at the door and before either could answer it, it opened. One look at the Brodys' expressions and it was clear they'd heard the argument right through the solid-oak partition. Their gazes slid from Rebecca to Alex and back again. Horrified understanding dawned in Kate's expression as she took in her friend's attire.

"Oh, no," she whispered, her grip tightening on her husband's arm.

Lance had taken in the situation with a single glance, as well. "Problem?" he asked coldly.

"No problem at all," Alex responded, keeping his gaze fixed on Rebecca. "A small misunderstanding that will be cleared up momentarily. Please come in and help yourself to some champagne." He addressed one of the catering staff who'd appeared in the doorway and indicated the tray. "Would you greet our guests as they arrive and show them to the ballroom? We'll join everyone in a minute."

He didn't wait for a response, but simply snagged Rebecca's arm and towed her in the direction of her quarters. Once there, he immediately went to the closet and removed the first bit of color and sparkle he came across, tossing it onto the bed. It pooled there in a brilliant lake of emerald-green silk.

"Strip," he ordered.

He wasn't surprised to see her mouth drop open in disbelief. "Have you lost your mind?" she stammered.

He managed to control his temper, but it was by a

mere thread. "Take off what you're wearing and put this dress on and do it within the next thirty seconds," he instructed, "or I swear by all that's holy, I'll do it for you."

Something about his implacable expression must have convinced her of his sincerity. She removed her blouse and skirt without a word of argument and in less than thirty seconds had exchanged it for the dress he'd chosen.

She lifted her chin and faced him. "Satisfied?"

"Not even a little." He regarded her critically. "Jewelry?"

Crossing to her dresser, she opened the top drawer and pulled out a rolled-up silk case tied with a tasseled string. After removing a few discreet pieces, she put them on. Pearls and gold gleamed softly against her earlobes and throat. "Now are we done?"

"One last thing." He came toward her, trying not to feel offended when she fell back a step. "Relax, Rebecca."

Reaching behind her, he removed the clip that held her hair in a tidy roll. The strands rained down to her shoulders, flashing with fire. He ran his fingers through the length, the silky texture tempting him almost beyond endurance. The emerald-green dress matched the color of her eyes and complemented the richness of her hair. Her anger had given her cheeks a healthy flush and made her beauty all the more startling.

"Now we're done," he informed her in a husky voice. "Let's go greet our guests."

"Your guests," she dared to correct.

"Our friends," he offered as a compromise.

She sighed. "I'm sorry." She rubbed her temples with her fingertips. "I guess I'm tired. I didn't mean to spoil the evening. It's just—" She broke off with a shake of her head. "Never mind. It doesn't matter."

He stilled. It should have occurred to him before that there was more going on than Rebecca being contrary. Or he would have if his anger hadn't gotten in the way. "Just what?"

She hesitated before admitting, "Someone said something to me about the party and about my role in it. I thought you expected me to show up as your housekeeper rather than a guest." She trailed off with a shrug. "Obviously I was wrong."

"Yes, you were. As was the person foolish enough to put the thought in your head. You should have asked me." He shook his head with a smile. "Or did your pride get in the way?"

"A Huntington flaw, it would seem." She returned his smile with a rueful one of her own. "One of many, in case you didn't notice."

"Can't say that I did," he lied diplomatically. He offered his arm. "Shall we?"

"My pleasure."

When they entered the ballroom, it was to find the rest of the guests had arrived and all eyes were fixed on them. For the first time in more years than he could recall, he felt the old awkwardness he used to experience when he'd been an angry outsider, new to a high school rife with the cream of the social select. Rebecca took one look at the expressions on the faces of her friends and offered an abashed grin.

"Sorry, guys. My fault. I misjudged the time I would need to change and get ready for the party."

Rebecca kept her hand firmly on his arm as she approached Darius and his wife, Summer, both of whom radiated the joy of a couple deeply in love and exquisitely blissful. She hugged first one and then the other. "Congratulations, you two. I couldn't be happier for you."

And just like that the entire atmosphere changed from charged to celebratory. The party continued on until the candles guttered and the caterers had long gone. Finally, sleepy couples offered their thanks and farewells, and just as the one day ended and the next began, the party drew to a close.

"That went well, don't you think?" At her nod of agreement, he gestured toward an unopened bottle of champagne. "Would you like a final drink before we turn in?"

Rebecca stifled a yawn. "Okay. Why don't we have it in the living room? I want to show you the tree we put up."

He poured two glasses of champagne and together they wandered into the room, a spacious area with a plush rug and thirty-foot ceilings trimmed in juniper. Floor-to-ceiling windows reflected the huge Christmas tree positioned in front of them. Alex let out a low whistle.

"I think that's the prettiest tree I've ever seen."

Rebecca smiled, amused to feel a blush warm her cheeks at the compliment. "Thanks."

"No." He turned to face her. "Thank you. You made this evening one of the most enjoyable I can remember in a long time."

"My pleasure."

He tossed back the champagne, all the time studying her. "What the hell am I going to do about you?"

She stilled and he saw her give the question serious consideration. Then she set her champagne aside and turned to him. Everything about her was vibrant and glowing. But it was her eyes that gave him the answer long before she spoke the words. "Love me," she whispered. "Make love to me right here and now."

"I've been giving that considerable thought," he admitted.

"And?"

"And no matter how hard I try, I can't keep myself from wanting you. From touching you." He placed his flute on a nearby table and gathered her into his arms. Then he lowered his head until their mouths were no more than a breath apart. "I can't keep from doing this…."

He kissed her, giving free rein to all that he'd kept under such tight control these past weeks. Her arms entwined around his neck and she shifted closer. From the very start she'd brought a delicate grace to their mating dance, melding their bodies with a slow, delicious rhythm so distinctively her own. It had always stunned him how she opened herself to him, completely and utterly, allowing him to know her at her most vulnerable. Gifting him—heart, body and soul—

without reluctance or reserve. And so it had been from the start.

The knowledge humbled him.

Without a word, he undressed first himself and then her, stripping away all artifice until all that remained was the bare essence of them both. As one, they sank onto the plush rug in front of the Christmas tree. The soft glow from the lights caressed her alabaster skin, sliding over the lovely swell of her breasts and setting aflame the burnished curls between her legs. Gently, he reached for her, the contrast between her paleness and his own bronzed skin tones adding to the dichotomy between masculine and feminine.

She was all light and brilliant color. A soft place to rest. He was made up of darkness, with the strength and determination of stone. He'd never been a soft place for her to rest and he doubted he ever would be. They were opposites in every way, coming together in brief, sweet interludes before fate pushed them apart again.

"Don't," she whispered.

He hesitated. "Do you want me to stop?" he asked, amazed by the depth of despair the request caused him.

She smiled. "Not that. Stop thinking. Stop analyzing." Her touch was one of infinite tenderness. "Stop trying to protect me and simply love me."

He didn't require any further prompting. Lowering his head, he worshipped her with mouth and tongue and teeth. He felt the warm tide of desire sweep across her skin like a sun-drenched wave, and he cupped her breast, feeling her heart beating for him and only him. She flowed against him, her hips lifting to mesh with his.

He took her with a slow, easy stroke, drawing the moment out. But the night wasn't meant for slow. A hunger burned between them, a demand that compelled them toward something harder and more urgent. Fierce heat melded with a fluid softness and he drove into her. Her breath escaped in a frantic plea as she lifted herself to him, matching his rhythm until they were both driven to a peak beyond anything he could recall ever experiencing before.

They teetered there for an instant. But it couldn't last, couldn't do more than hold them there for a brief, incandescent moment before they took flight, soaring together, forever bound. He surrendered to the woman in his arms, surrendered all he'd worked so hard to protect. Surrendered his body and heart.

Surrendered all that he was to the woman he loved.

The next morning Rebecca awoke to find herself in her own bed. She stretched, feeling happier and more deeply in love than she could ever remember. Anything and everything seemed possible. Life was perfect—or so it seemed—right up until she arrived at the Texas Cattleman's Club to have lunch with Kate. She caught a buzz of excitement the instant she stepped through the doors, one that increased when she walked into view.

For some reason, she was the center of attention and

it made her extremely nervous. It only strengthened when she caught a glimpse of her friend's broad, excited grin. Kate flew to her side and threw her arms around Rebecca.

"Congratulations! All I can say is that it's about damn time."

"What? What's happened?"

"Don't play coy. Not with me. Come on." She held out her hand in a demanding manner. "Let's see it."

Rebecca shook her head in genuine bewilderment. "I don't have a clue what you're talking about. See what?"

"The rock Alex put on your finger last night."

Rebecca's mouth dropped open. *"What?"*

Kate froze, her eyes widening. Hustling Rebecca into the club library, she dragged her to a secluded reading alcove. "You need to level with me, Bec. Are you or are you not engaged to Alex?"

Rebecca's throat closed over. "Not."

"Well, your father is here having lunch with some of his cronies. Someone made some crack about your serving Alex's guests at the party last night and your father told everyone within hearing that you and Alex are engaged."

"No." Rebecca shook her head, her voice taking on an air of desperation. "No, that's not true."

"Well, you better get it straightened out and fast. Like, seriously fast."

"Why? Oh, no. Tell me Alex isn't here, too."

"Not yet. But the guys are meeting so Darius can update them about the arson investigation. And if he hasn't gotten wind of this yet, he will the minute he steps foot through the front doors."

Rebecca shot to her feet. "Where's my father?"

"He's just finishing lunch at the café."

She left the library without another word and caught up with her father just as he was exiting the restaurant. Grabbing his arm, she drew him away from the avid gaze of the other patrons. "Kate just told me you announced to everyone that I'm engaged to Alex. Where did you hear such a thing, Dad? It's not true and you have to tell everyone it's not."

"It will be," her father retorted calmly. "Montoya can't very well back out now that it's public information, not without looking like a total bastard."

"You set us up? Deliberately?" Rebecca demanded in an appalled undertone. "How could you do such a thing?"

His jaw assumed a stubborn slant. "I've only told everyone what I had to in order for us to continue holding our heads up in this town."

"Have you lost your mind? After everything Alex has done for us—"

"What he's done for us?" her father repeated in an irate undertone. "What he's done is turn you into a laughingstock. He's forced you to become both his housekeeper and his mistress."

"In case you failed to notice, I've chosen my own path in life, Dad, just as you have. Alex didn't force me to do anything. *I* went to *him* and told him I'd be his housekeeper until I paid off your debt. He didn't want me working for him and for good reason. I'm a terrible housekeeper. And if I ended up in his bed, it was because that's where I wanted to be."

He waved her comments aside as though they didn't matter. "You're a fool, Rebecca. You could work for that man for the rest of your life and never come close to putting a dent in that debt."

"What are you talking about? Three hundred thousand is a lot, granted, but I've already paid down a decent portion of that."

"It's not three hundred thousand. It's one-point-three *million*. My debt to Rodriquez? It's a million dollars, Rebecca."

Her mouth dropped open and she could only stare, stricken. To her horror, Alex chose that moment to appear, his expression one of unmitigated fury. He could barely bring himself to look at her.

Focusing on her father, he said, "I'll deal with you in the morning when I'm not tempted to put an end to your miserable life. And in case you've forgotten, your membership was suspended. I suggest you leave before I have you thrown out." He still refused to so much as glance her way, even when he addressed her. "Rebecca, we're leaving. Let's go."

He didn't bother to see whether she followed. Before going after him, she addressed her father in a harsh undertone. "Fair warning, Dad. When Alex is done with you, I intend to have a go at whatever he hasn't chewed up and spat out."

"It was for your own good."

Rebecca refused to let him get away with that one. "No, Dad. It was for yours."

She caught up with Alex just as he exited the club and addressed him in a breathless voice. "I'm so sorry. I promise I'll straighten it out. I had no idea he planned to do that."

"We'll discuss it back at the ranch."

They covered the miles in a painful silence. His anger was so great he practically vibrated with it. She could only hope the time it took to reach El Diablo allowed his infamous temper to cool somewhat. It was a forlorn hope. She joined him as he pounded up the steps of the porch and entered the house. He made a beeline for his office where he poured several fingers of whiskey into a tumbler and downed it in a single swallow.

"Madre de Dios!" he swore. "I have had about as much as I can stomach."

"I'm sorry," she said again. "I promise I'll take care of it."

He poured two drinks this time, then rounded on her. "How do you intend to do that?" He handed her one of the glasses. "'My mistake, everyone. Alex didn't propose. My father just claimed he did because he couldn't bear the idea that I've become both his housekeeper and mistress.' Is that what you plan to say?"

"Something like that." She took a gulp of the whiskey and winced. The potent liquor burned her throat and caused tears to fill her eyes. She much preferred whiskey when it was disguised as Irish coffee. "I may leave out the housekeeper and mistress part of the explanation," she managed to gasp.

"Do not attempt to humor me. I don't find any part of this the least bit amusing."

She released a tired sigh. "I don't, either, Alex. But considering all that's happened over the past few weeks, a sense of humor is just about the only thing left to me." He started to speak, but she waved him silent. "What does it matter what I tell people or what they think of me? They can't think much worse than they already do."

"But they can think worse of me."

It took her a moment to puzzle through that one. And then it hit her. "And they'd think worse of you if you married the daughter of a thief and arsonist, wouldn't they, Alex?"

She must have hit pretty close to the truth because he swore again, this time a virulent string of words in Spanish. All the while Rebecca fought to breathe. To pretend that his attitude toward her and her father hadn't wounded her to the very depths of her being. To her relief, fury came to her rescue.

"Let me make sure I understand this," she said with impressive calm. "You're not upset because of what my father did, but because you're—" she struggled to find the most appropriate word "—because you're disgusted at the idea of being romantically linked to a Huntington? Your business would be harmed? Your precious reputation? Your honor?"

His head jerked up as though scenting danger. Took him long enough, she thought. "Rebecca—"

"Just answer the question, Alex." She tossed back the whiskey, this time ignoring the alcoholic burn, and slammed the glass onto his desk so hard she couldn't believe it didn't shatter. "On second thought, never mind. You've already made your feelings crystal clear."

He studied her without expression. "It's not you. You understand that, don't you? It's your father."

"No, I got it. I'm good enough to bed, so long as no one finds out. But you wouldn't dream of marrying me."

He cocked an eyebrow. "Is that what you were hoping would happen? I'd take you to bed and fall in love with you again? We'd marry and your father's debts would be miraculously forgiven?"

"In other words, did I seduce you as some sort of nefarious plot so you'd pay off our debts and save my father from jail? Sure, Alex. Have it your way." She closed the distance between them. "Now let me ask you a question. When I approached you about taking over as your housekeeper in order to pay off our debt, why didn't you tell me it was an impossibility? A one-point-three-million-dollar impossibility? Or would that have spoiled your fun at having the opportunity to turn the tables on the Huntingtons and get a little payback after all?"

"Your father told you?" At her nod, he sighed. "Interesting, considering I promised him I would remain silent on the issue. I did warn you the debt couldn't be settled anytime soon."

"There were alternatives to telling me, Alex. If you'd flat-out refused to hire me, there's not much I could have done to force your agreement."

He shrugged. "I thought having you stay at El Diablo might protect you from Rodriquez."

It made a hideous sort of sense. "So it had nothing to do with wanting me back in your bed?"

He didn't answer that, but she could see the truth in his eyes. He wanted her. He'd always wanted her, just as she'd always wanted him. What a sad pair they were. Exhaustion swamped her.

"I'll pack my things and be out of your life first thing in the morning." A bit melodramatic, but maybe he'd put that down to the amount of whiskey she'd consumed. She paused by the door, but couldn't bring herself to look at him again in case she burst into tears. "You know…I find it interesting that you've always held my father in such contempt when you've spent your entire life turning yourself into an exact replica of him. And just in case you were wondering, tonight you completed the transformation. You're just as much a snob as he ever was."

And with that, she walked out.

Ten

The ringing of her cell phone woke Rebecca from a groggy sleep. Sitting up in bed, she looked around her room in a daze while the events of the previous night crashed down on her. At some point in the midst of her packing frenzy she must have fallen asleep, leaving the evidence of those crazed hours strewn around her. Clothing was piled half in and half out of suitcases. Dresser drawers hung open. And the closet door stood agape, with the hangers stripped bare.

The cell phone continued its annoying chirp and she cleared her throat as she fumbled to answer it, praying it was Alex calling with a change of heart. Though why he would call instead of simply joining her in bed…

"Yes, hello?"

"Good morning, señorita. I trust you slept well last night?"

She hesitated for a full ten seconds before moistening her lips and replying. "Paulo?"

"Very good," he responded with warm approval. "You've come to recognize my voice. An excellent step forward in our relationship. Soon you'll learn to listen to my every word, and of course, always do exactly as I tell you."

Was he kidding? "That's not likely."

"Really?" His laughter sent a chill of dread coursing through her. "I think it's not only likely, but inevitable. Why don't we test my theory and see. Are you listening, *muñequita?*"

She vaguely recalled that meant *little doll,* but suspected it had a slightly different connotation the way he chose to use it. "I'm listening."

"See, already part of my prediction has come true." His voice lowered, became more sinister. "Let's see if I can't make the rest come true, as well. Shall we try?"

Her palms grew damp, making it difficult to hold the cell phone. "What do you want?"

"I want you to come to Huntington Manor. Alone. When you get here, you will join your father and me for a little…conversation."

Her heart leaped. "My father?" she repeated.

"Is right here with me. Shall I put him on?"

"Yes. Yes, I want to speak to him."

"Very well. I will allow it. This time."

There was a momentary pause and she could hear men's voices conversing in the background. Then her father came on the line. "Gentry's here! Find Alex. Tell him—"

Her father broke off with a groan and then Rodriquez spoke again. "If you are very wise, you won't listen to your father. He's an old man. He can't handle pressure well. Such pressure could do him serious harm. Do we understand one another?"

Terror filled her. What had he already done to her father to cause him to groan like that? What more was he willing to do if she didn't follow his instructions? Injecting a docile tone into her voice that was only partially feigned, she said, "Don't hurt him. Please, Paulo."

To her relief, it worked. "Much better. I like how you ask so nicely." He paused a beat before continuing. "It's time for you to come home. Get into your car and drive over here. Then the three of us—"

"Don't you mean four?"

He chuckled. "Very well. The *four* of us will have a brief conversation while we determine the future direction of our relationship." The amusement faded from his voice. "Under no circumstances will you call Alex. Besides, I've arranged for him to be well occupied at his office with strict instructions not to be disturbed. He won't be able to help you, even if he were so inclined. Do you understand?"

"Yes."

"Excellent. See? I told you that you'd listen and obey me. I'm very pleased at how quickly you've learned. You won't keep your future husband waiting, will you, Rebecca?"

She gritted her teeth. "No, Paulo," she answered dutifully.

"See that you don't."

The instant he disconnected the call, she began to punch in Alex's number, then hesitated. She'd never been a good liar and doubted she could fool Paulo if he asked her whether or not she'd disobeyed him. But she hadn't promised she wouldn't call someone else. Unfortunately, this time she doubted anyone could save her from what Paulo had planned.

Again, she started to use her cell, but thought better of it. Allowing instinct to drive her, she called Kate using Alex's landline. Precious moments passed while she argued with her best friend, finally hanging up in a panic when she realized how much time was passing. Running flat-out for the pickup truck she'd purchased to replace her Cabriolet, she turned the key in the ignition and prayed that the stubborn engine would turn over. To her relief, it caught on the first try. Grinding it into gear, she bumped her way down Alex's gravel entryway.

The drive from El Diablo to Huntington Manor seemed interminable. When she finally arrived everything looked perfectly normal, with the exception of a powerful black vehicle squatting on the grass in front of the house like some predatory cockroach. No doubt cutting across the lawn was Rodriquez's quaint manner of marking the territory he intended to claim. Gathering her self-control, she climbed the steps and entered the house.

She suspected she'd find her father entertaining their "guests" in the library. Her guess proved accurate. She entered to find her father seated at a desk with his ex-foreman and Paulo Rodriquez standing over him while he scratched his signature on a piece of paper.

Rodriquez looked up at her entrance and offered her a look of cool approval. "Join the party, *muñequita*. We've been waiting for you."

"What's going on?" She focused her attention on the wad of papers in front of her father. "What is my father signing?"

"Just a few unimportant documents."

Right. Sure they were. "Let me guess. Unimportant documents that transfer ownership of Huntington Manor over to you?"

He grinned and shook his finger at her. "I can't fool you, can I?" His smile faded and he approached, holding out his hand. "Your cell phone, if you don't mind."

Her fingers tightened on the strap of her purse. "I do mind."

"Do not attempt to play with me, señorita. I am most displeased with you right now."

She attempted to swallow her fear, but her throat had gone bone dry. Removing the phone from her purse, she passed it into Rodriquez's keeping. "Why do you need my cell?"

He flipped it open and pressed a series of buttons. "I wish to see who you've phoned since we last spoke." He nodded in approval. "Very good. No calls were placed after mine."

"Satisfied?"

"Not yet. But soon. Come." He waved a hand toward the couch as though he were the host and she his guest. "Make yourself comfortable. You won't be going anywhere for a very long time. You and I... Let's just say we have plans to discuss."

Her sense of dread increased and she forced herself to bury it beneath an air of casual inquisitiveness. "What sort of plans?"

He deliberately waited a beat, no doubt in an effort to increase the apprehension she'd failed to conceal from him. "Why, wedding plans, of course."

"I'm going in there and nothing any of you say or do is going to stop me," Alex stated implacably.

"Don't be more of an idiot than you can help, Montoya," Lance Brody argued. "That's precisely what Rodriquez is counting on. Then he'll have all of you."

Alex stared at Huntington Manor, standing tall and stately in the distance while he remained tucked out of sight like some timid mouse cowering before a hungry cat. "I'm not going to allow Rebecca to remain in there unprotected."

"Will he be armed?" Darius cut in.

"Without question."

Darius lifted an eyebrow. "So, what? You're just going to stroll in and tell him to let your woman go? Once he has the two of you together, he'll use you against each other."

Lance took up the argument. "I know Becca as well as anyone. You would put yourself in harm's way to protect her—she'll do the same on your behalf. And you damn well know it. Think. You can't give Rodriquez that sort of leverage."

"I have to."

"You're not in this alone," Lance maintained. He nodded toward the rest of the men grouped around them. His brother, Mitch, had his back. Alex's future brother-in-law, Justin Dupree, had positioned himself on one side, while Kevin Novak had taken up the other. "We're all here for you. Every last man."

Alex found it difficult to reply. He'd been alone for so long, it was hard to accept that was no longer the case. "Thank you," he said simply.

"Here's the deal," Darius said, laying it out. "If we storm the place, chances are someone will get hurt. Or Rodriquez will claim he was there at Huntington's invitation. We don't have any evidence to prove differently. We sure as hell don't have any evidence that he's guilty of any crime. There's no proof that he scammed Huntington. No proof that he intends anyone any harm. He'll walk."

"Then what am I—are *we*—supposed to do?" Alex demanded in frustration.

Darius grinned. "I thought you'd never ask."

* * *

Rebecca glared at Rodriquez. "You can't honestly believe I'll agree to marry you?"

"You will unless you want to see your father put in jail as an arsonist."

She switched her gaze to Gentry. "He can't testify against my father without implicating himself."

Rodriquez waved that aside. "Cornelius is about to take a long, restful trip. But before he goes, he'll leave behind more than enough evidence to convict your father of the charges." He approached the couch and ran a finger along the curve of her cheek, his mouth tightening at her involuntary flinch. "Soon you will not just welcome my touch, but beg for it."

"Take your hands off her," Sebastian roared from where he sat behind his desk. He half rose, but Gentry shoved him back into the chair.

Rodriquez shot him a look of disgust. "Shut up, old man. You have your own problems to worry about." He took a seat beside Rebecca and gathered her hands in his. "Don't look so tragic, *muñequita*. We're going to have a perfect life together. We will be a happily married couple and share this estate. I will stamp my own name on the history of the Huntingtons, improve on what your father began. You will fall madly in love with me and be the most beautiful bride anyone has ever seen."

She shook her head, tears gathering in her eyes. "No. Never."

He ignored her, speaking with surprising tenderness.

"Can't you picture it, my sweet? We will start our own dynasty, one to rival all others in Maverick County. People will see how we live and envy us. Envy all that I have managed to acquire. Me, a poor nobody from the barrio, now the richest, most powerful man in the county." His hand settled low on her stomach, splaying across her abdomen in a possessive gesture. "In time, you will grow heavy with the first of our many children. Children who will go to the finest schools and have friends among the most elite in Somerset."

Before she could tell him just what she thought of his insane dream, someone cleared his throat. Jerking free of Rodriquez's hold, she saw Alex standing in the doorway, leaning against the doorjamb. Her heart leaped at the sight, while her stomach twisted into knots. She'd known by calling Kate that she risked Alex storming Huntington Manor, but she'd hoped he'd show more sense than to play into Rodriquez's hands by simply walking right in.

"Am I interrupting something?" he asked with seeming casualness.

Rodriquez shot to his feet, his hand darting behind his back where she saw the butt of a sleek, black gun. "What the hell are you doing here, Montoya?" he demanded. His infuriated gaze switched from Alex to Rebecca. "I warned you not to call him. I warned you!"

She looked him straight in the eye and spoke the God's honest truth, praying he'd believe her. "I didn't. I swear I didn't."

"You can believe her," Alex said in a calm voice, drawing the other man's attention. "I'm only here to deliver the rest of Rebecca's belongings. We had a... I guess you could call it a falling-out last night. Bottom line is, she quit. Since Her Highness was taking her sweet time getting her backside out of my house, I thought I'd help move her along."

"She was leaving you?" A hint of uncertainty threaded through Rodriquez's voice. "Why would she do that?"

"Let's just say she refused to fulfill all her duties as my housekeeper and I got fed up waiting for her to change her mind."

To Rebecca's amazement, Rodriquez bought it, his expression one of sheer elation. "She wouldn't sleep with you?"

Alex shrugged, and a hint of irritation drifted across his face. "It happens."

"But the rumors around town..."

"I have my pride, Paulo," Alex snapped. "People thought what I wanted them to think."

"You son of a bitch!" Sebastian burst out. "How dare you ruin my daughter's reputation?"

"And how dare you tell everyone we were engaged," Alex shot back.

"Enough," Rodriquez interrupted. His suspicious gaze darted from person to person before swinging back in Alex's direction. "You've delivered Rebecca's belongings. Feel free to leave, Montoya."

"No problem." Then he hesitated. "Although..."

"Although what?"

A deep scowl blossomed on Alex's face. "I've been thinking about what you said when you came to visit me the other day."

Rodriquez bristled. "You mean when you tried to take all of this away from me?"

Alex gave a chagrined shrug. "Foolish, I know. I've never been able to beat you at anything. I don't know why I even bother trying."

Clearly mollified, Rodriquez nodded. "It's time you learned how pointless it is."

"You're right. So, it's only fair that I—" he grimaced as though the words left a bitter taste in his mouth "—congratulate you for a game well played."

Rodriquez smiled. "You never saw it coming, did you, *amigo?*"

A hint of admiration gleamed in Alex's eyes. "You must have had this planned a long time to pull it off so successfully."

To Rebecca's horror, El Gato stiffened. "I have no idea what you're talking about. I've planned nothing."

Alex crinkled his brow in bewilderment. "What? Oh, I don't mean…" He gestured toward her father and the papers strewn across the desk. "Whatever you have going on there is none of my business. If I could have figured a way to fleece Huntington with no one being the wiser, I'd have done it myself. No, I'm talking about Rebecca."

"The woman?" Rodriquez glanced her way and wet

his lips before jerking his attention back to Alex. "I have wanted her for a long time."

"I didn't realize how much or I wouldn't have interfered." He advanced into the room, just a single pace, his hands at his sides, his shoulders slightly hunched in defeat. "But you couldn't take her when she and I first started dating, could you?"

Rodriquez shrugged. "Not so long as she was with you." His chin lifted defiantly. "I stuck to the code. You can't claim otherwise."

"True." Alex's mouth tightened. "You wouldn't have taken her from me. But if you could trick us to part ways…"

"That's a different story, isn't it?"

"So you told everyone that I'd seduced her as part of a bet."

"You figured that one out, yes?" Rodriquez's smile widened in delight. "One of my more clever ideas, I must admit."

"But you also knew she'd need a little incentive to fall into your arms. That's when you hit on your investment scheme. As much as I hate to admit it, it was brilliant." Alex's scowl returned. "In fact, I wish I'd thought of it myself."

To Rebecca's relief, aside from a low growl, her father remained silent. She shot him a warning look.

"As I told you before," Rodriquez said. "The greedy pig couldn't get enough. Even when the investments went under, he came back for more. It was so easy to set up."

"Serves him right," Alex murmured.

"Exactly! He deserves everything coming to him." Rodriquez gestured around him. "Soon all his possessions will become mine, including his daughter."

"You were right, you know," Alex admitted. "If I hadn't been so preoccupied with having Rebecca again, I'd have been on board a lot sooner. Just think of it, Paulo. A pair of *hermanos* from the barrio owning two of the richest spreads in all of Maverick County. We'll be members in the same club, rubbing elbows with people who years ago wouldn't have given us the time of day."

"And the woman?" Rodriquez demanded through narrowed eyes. "What of her?"

Alex grinned. "She's all yours. You've earned her as your reward."

Triumph glowed in Rodriquez's dark eyes. "Yes, I have, haven't I?"

"There's just one thing I don't get." He gave a self-deprecating shrug. "I guess my mind just doesn't work like yours."

"It never did."

"And never will," Alex conceded.

"Tell me what you don't understand. I will explain it to you," Rodriquez offered expansively.

"I just don't get the arson fires. Why the hell did Huntington have Gentry set them? Were they just a distraction, so all the club members would be at each other's throats?"

A flash of anger exploded across Rodriquez's face and Rebecca went perfectly still, terror creeping up her spine. "You think that *cabrón* has the intelligence to plan something like that? You insult me!"

Alex's eyebrows shot upward in amazement. "*You* planned the arson fires? You had Gentry set them?" His anger rose to match Rodriquez's. "You burned down my barn? What the hell for?"

"To set Huntington up. To give me extra leverage when the time came to close my trap around him." Paulo attempted to placate his friend. "I apologize, *amigo*. I wouldn't have done such a thing to you if it hadn't been absolutely necessary."

Alex steamed for a few seconds before shrugging it off. "I suppose if you can let bygones be bygones, so can I," he said grudgingly.

"Agreed." He wagged a finger in Alex's direction. "I did not like being at odds with you. Don't let it happen again."

"You're right. My mistake." He closed the distance between them and offered his hand. "What do you say we start over."

Paulo grinned and gripped Alex's hand. "I'd like that."

The instant the two men connected, Alex's left hand plowed into Rodriquez's jaw, the movement so fast it was little more than a blur. El Gato's eyes rolled into the back of his head and he dropped like a stone, out cold. Before Gentry could do more than jerk to attention, Sebastian snatched the burl wood lamp off his desk and smashed it over the top of his ex-foreman's head. Then he turned to glare at Alex.

"I hope to hell you're wearing a wire, Montoya."

"That's Mr. Montoya to you. And yes. I'm wearing a wire."

Sebastian's jaw worked for a moment then to Rebecca's shock, he nodded. "Mr. Montoya. I'm man enough to admit when I've made a mistake. I've been wrong about you and wrong in my treatment of you and your family." He crossed the room and stuck out his hand. "I know I don't deserve it, but I hope you'll accept my apology."

Alex hesitated for a split second before taking Sebastian's hand in a firm shake. Then he turned to Rebecca. For a long moment he simply looked at her. Then he opened his arms. With an inarticulate cry she exploded from the couch and threw herself against him. He held her in a grip that spoke of pain and love and relief, all wrapped up in one.

"I'm also man enough to admit when I've made a mistake," he whispered against her hair. "I'm sorry, *dulzura*. I was wrong the other night. About everything."

"And the bet? You never had a bet with Rodriguez?"

"Never." Tenderness filled his expression. "I could never do such a thing to you."

Tears filled her eyes. "I should have known. Maybe if I hadn't been so young and foolish, I would have."

Suddenly the room was crowded with people. "You do know you're still being recorded, right?" Darius Franklin asked drily.

Alex never took his gaze off Rebecca. "So long as you have Sebastian Huntington's apology on tape and make me a half dozen copies, I don't give a damn."

And then he lowered his head and kissed her. Kissed her world right. Kissed his way home. Kissed her with all the passion of a man who understood where his heart lay and with whom. When they finally pulled back, it was to discover the room deserted.

He cupped her face, his thumbs sweeping away tears she hadn't even realized she'd cried. "I love you, Becca. I have since the moment we first met."

"And I love you." She hesitated, one final cloud casting a shadow on her happiness. "You realize your reputation will be linked with mine and my father's?"

"I was a fool," he said simply. "And I'm more sorry than I can possibly express. I'd be honored to have my name linked with yours and be part of your family."

It was all she needed to hear. With a contented sigh, she surrendered to the inevitable…a life with Alex, filled with laughter, passion beyond imagining and a love that would last them for the rest of their lives. "Take me home, Alex."

He swept her into his arms, allowing love to wash away the bitterness of the past and provide a pathway toward their future. "I thought you'd never ask."

Epilogue

The small mission church was crowded to capacity, the beautiful stone building decorated for the Christmas Eve wedding ceremony in fresh greenery and red and white roses that combined their perfume with the delicate scent of candle wax. A soft prelude echoed off the walls and rafters as Alicia and Justin's bridal party made its way down the aisle.

Cara, in her role as matron of honor, reached the altar just as the sweet herald of the Trumpet Voluntary sounded. And then Alicia appeared, glorious in a fitted ivory gown that swept into a long train. She clung to her brother's arm, tears glistening from beneath the beautiful lace mantilla-style veil that framed her exquisite features. Beside her, Alex looked more handsome than Rebecca had ever seen him. While all eyes were riveted on his sister, his gaze never wavered from hers.

Once he'd given away the bride in traditional fashion, he crossed to where Rebecca was seated in the front pew. As the clock edged from Christmas Eve toward Christmas Day, the ceremony proceeded at a stately pace.

Through it all, Alex held her hand, their fingers interlaced. It couldn't have been more perfect. While Justin and Alicia exchanged their vows, their love for one another unmistakable, the other couples who'd recently found a love just as deep and enduring exchanged looks of joy and passion. And then it was over. The newly married couple shared a lingering kiss while tears of happiness glistened in the eyes of those who watched.

Trumpets began the recessional, the familiar strands of Ode to Joy accompanying the bridal party's departure. While the guests began a general exodus of the church, Alex gathered Rebecca into his arms.

"It's been a long, hard road for us, hasn't it, *dulzura?*"

"At times," she conceded.

"Maybe because it's been so hard, it makes this moment so much more meaningful."

She smiled and asked, "This moment? Why this moment?"

"Listen." Around them the bells tolled the midnight hour. "It's the first minute of Christmas and my final responsibility to my family has been discharged." He took her hand in his and slipped a ring onto her finger. "I can't think of a better time to tell you that I love you more than life itself and to ask if you'll marry me."

A gorgeous diamond solitaire captured the flickering candlelight and threw it outward in rainbow rays of hope. "Oh, Alex." It took her a moment to gather her self-control enough to respond. "I've loved you since the minute I first saw you."

His gaze grew tender. "Is that a yes?"

She answered him with a kiss, a kiss that held all the passion their life together would bring and echoed the love that had filled the church that evening. When she pulled back, the expression in her eyes was beyond anything he'd ever see before.

"Yes, Alex. It's definitely a yes."

* * * * *

*Bestselling author Lynne Graham is back
with a fabulous new trilogy!*

PREGNANT BRIDES

Three ordinary girls—naive, but also honest and plucky...
*Three fabulously wealthy, impossibly handsome
and very ruthless men...*
*When opposites attract and passion leads to pregnancy...
it can only mean marriage!*
*Available next month from Harlequin Presents®:
the first installment*

DESERT PRINCE, BRIDE OF INNOCENCE

* * *

'THIS EVENING I'm flying to New York for two weeks,'
Jasim imparted with a casualness that made her heart sink
like a stone. 'That's why I had you brought here. I own this
apartment and you'll be comfortable here while I'm abroad.'

'I can afford my own accommodation although I may not
need it for long. I'll have another job by the time you
get back—'

Jasim released a slightly harsh laugh. 'There's no need for
you to look for another position. How would I ever see you?
Don't you understand what I'm offering you?'

Elinor stood very still. 'No, I must be incredibly thick
because I haven't quite worked out yet what you're offering
me....'

His charismatic smile slashed his lean dark visage.
'Naturally, I want to take care of you....'

HPEX0110A

'No, thanks.' Elinor forced a smile and mentally willed him not to demean her with some sordid proposition. 'The only man who will ever take *care* of me with my agreement will be my husband. I'm willing to wait for you to come back but I'm not willing to be kept by you. I'm a very independent woman and what I give, I give freely.'

Jasim frowned. 'You make it all sound so serious.'

'What happened between us last night left pure chaos in its wake. Right now, I don't know whether I'm on my head or my heels. I'll stay for a while because I have nowhere else to go in the short term. So maybe it's good that you'll be away for a while.'

Jasim pulled out his wallet to extract a card. 'My private number,' he told her, presenting her with it as though it was a precious gift, which indeed it was. Many women would have done just about anything to gain access to that direct hotline to him, but his staff guarded his privacy with scrupulous care.

Before he could close the wallet, his blood ran cold in his veins. How could he have made such a serious oversight? What if he had got her pregnant? He knew that an unplanned pregnancy would engulf his life like an avalanche, crush his freedom and suffocate him. He barely stilled a shudder at the threat of such an outcome and thought how ironic it was that what his older brother had longed and prayed for to secure the line to the throne should strike Jasim as an absolute disaster....

* * *

What will proud Prince Jasim do if Elinor is expecting his royal baby? Perhaps an arranged marriage is the only solution! But will Elinor agree? Find out in DESERT PRINCE, BRIDE OF INNOCENCE by Lynne Graham [#2884], available from Harlequin Presents® in January 2010.

Silhouette *Desire*

KINGS OF THE BOARDROOM

*They rule their empire with an iron fist...but
need the right women to melt their steel-cold hearts!*

The Ad Man: Jason Reagert

*His new campaign: wedding bands—for the man
who needs to get the ring on her finger...fast!*

What's an executive to do when his one-night
stand is pregnant and his new client hates scandal?
Propose a temporary marriage, of course. Yet their
sizzling passion is anything but temporary....

Look for

BOSSMAN'S BABY SCANDAL

by

CATHERINE MANN

Available January

Always Powerful, Passionate and Provocative.

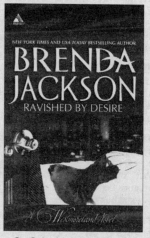

Silhouette *Desire*

COMING NEXT MONTH
Available January 12, 2010

#1987 FROM PLAYBOY TO PAPA!—Leanne Banks
Man of the Month
Surprised to learn he has a son, he's even more surprised to learn his ex-lover's sister is raising the boy. When he demands the child live with him, he agrees to let her come too…as his wife.

#1988 BOSSMAN'S BABY SCANDAL—Catherine Mann
Kings of the Boardroom
What's an executive to do when his one-night stand is pregnant and his new client hates scandal? Propose a temporary marriage, of course. Yet their sizzling passion is anything but temporary….

#1989 TEMPTING THE TEXAS TYCOON—Sara Orwig
He'll receive five million dollars if he marries within the year—and a sexy business rival provides the perfect opportunity. But she refuses to submit to his desires…especially when she discovers his reasons.

**#1990 AFFAIR WITH THE REBEL HEIRESS—
Emily McKay**
Known for his conquests in the boardroom—and the bedroom—the CEO isn't about to let his latest fling stand in his way. He'll acquire her company, wild passion or not. Though he soon finds out she has other plans in mind….

**#1991 THE MAGNATE'S PREGNANCY PROPOSAL—
Sandra Hyatt**
She came to tell him the in vitro worked—she was carrying his late brother's baby. When he drops the bomb that her baby is actually *his,* he'll stop at nothing to stake his claim. Will she let him claim *her?*

#1992 CLAIMING HIS BOUGHT BRIDE—Rachel Bailey
To meet the terms of his inheritance, he convinces her to marry him. But can he seduce her into being his wife more than just on paper?

SDCNMBPA1209